Examinations of Paradise
Book 2

THE
LOST
PATROL

Cold Death in Paradise

THE
LOST
PATROL

Cold Death in Paradise

John Holt

ABSOLUTELY AMAZING eBOOKS

ABSOLUTELY AMAZING eBOOKS

Published by Whiz Bang LLC, 926 Truman Avenue, Key West, Florida 33040, USA.

For information contact:
Publisher@AbsolutelyAmazingEbooks.com

ISBN-13: 978-1945772009 (Absolutely Amazing Ebooks)
ISBN-10: 194577200X

For Danny O'Keefe

THE
LOST
PATROL

Cold Death in Paradise

INTRODUCTION

THIS BOOK WAS TRIGGERED by the Northwest Mounted Police's infamous Lost Patrol that met with disaster during the winter of 1910-11 while traveling in Canada's Yukon and Northwest territories. Ever since I first heard of the fate of the patrol I've been fascinated by not only what happened to these men, but in what is waiting for any of us who venture into the Arctic wilderness. Doing research at the museum in Dawson City some years ago, Yukon further set the hook. Events in this book are fictitious. Any resemblance to actual persons, living or dead, or actual events, past or present, is coincidental. Characters in this novel whose traits are loosely based on individuals living in the Arctic north country during the period of 1895-1911 are fictitious. Some scenes in the book, while similar to recorded activities of this time period, are also fictitious and are sequenced by the author's whim or need to facilitate his curious notion of narrative arc. Use of terms that include "Indian," "aboriginal," "Loucheaux," and the like, while no doubt at times politically incorrect today, were in common use at the time this book took place, so they are used in the narrative for temporal verisimilitude. When creating and describing natural places in this book, I drew from the experiences of the numerous trips to the Yukon and Northwest territories that I've made in past years. I am indebted to the excellent research author Dick North has done on this subject.

- John Holt
Livingston, Montana
February 2016

Have you swept the visioned valley with
The green stream streaking through it,
Searched the Vastness for something you have lost?
Have you strung your soul to silence?
Then for God's sake go and do it;
Hear the challenge, learn the lesson, pay the cost.

- From *"The Call of the Wild"* by Robert W. Service

-CHAPTER ONE-

"In the event of my demise, all money in my leather satchel stored at Herschel Island headquarters, and bank accounts, clothes, etc., I leave to those I have served with in the Northwest Mounted Police. To those I am honored to call my friends. God bless all."
- Inspector Wallams Macdonald,
RNWMP
November 1910

HE HAS NO WAY OF KNOWING how many yards it is to the summit of the pass from where he is lying far out here in the middle of the brutal, shrieking weather that is the anthem of winter above the Arctic Circle.

Is the distance to the path down the other side of these mountains within his grasp or is it much farther than he can imagine or is capable of traversing? Inspector Wallams Macdonald of the Northwest Mounted Police is past the point of caring or even noticing the bitter cold. His patrol is fighting a withering battle against minus seventy degree temperatures, blizzards, fierce winds, starvation, and the abject desperation that comes from being stranded in country so untamed, so unexplored as to seem unworldly. He and the other Mounties have trudged and pushed through dense stands of trees, clinging brush and across snow encrusted sweeps of shattered rock, and hung on to the sheer edges of limestone precipices like men who fear that they may be doomed to this ice-bound hell for eternity if they don't keep grinding onward. His mind is numbed, staggered. His hands and feet are frozen stumps, the skin turned a ragged red and black from extreme frostbite. Surviving another day, an hour, the next minute is the force that drives him now.

The wind slams down the steep slopes of the mountains that form this glacial cirque. Barren peaks flash in and out of dark gray-silver clouds made from plumes of ice crystals streaming from the summits like ghosts for hundreds of yards as the gale screams both above him in an almost subliminal wail and into his chest as the gale cuts down below through the dwarf trees in an unfiltered roar. The air smells of polar cold and nothing else. No faint scent of pine, earth or water. The land is locked up. Frozen granite hard. Waves of snow swirl through the forest and across the ice-bound stream thousands of feet below him, or they form tight spirals that tear into the storm-battered trees scattering pine needles and branches. Caribou, moose, grizzly, wolverine, eagle, all of them are vanished like they never lived in the land. There are less than four hours of daylight at this time of year, and that is only a dull illumination like that of a dangerous dusk edged by a soft silver glow to the south while directly above him is the darkness of night that has already enveloped him. Billions of stars and spiral galaxies, arcing planets and the northern lights burn above him with a constancy that seems insane. The aurora swirls and whips in the solar wind. Fluorescent shades of pink, orange, green and delicate blue light the landscape with ethereal ripplings of color. The universe shines through all of this with an intensity that is bright enough to cast shadows from protruding hunks of sharply eroding rock. The dark shapes thrown by the stone dance grimly about him appearing to be driven by the wind.

Macdonald struggles to rise from his hands and knees, a difficult task because of days of near starvation. The pain is constant and extreme. His awful companion now. He crawls along the rock to Corporal John Galpin whose responsibility is to guide the Inspector and his party through the ragged mountains and barren winter tundra of the Yukon and Northwest Territories. Has his assignment ended in failure? Will the patrol fail to reach Dawson City? Will all of them die? Constable R.G. McConnell is down far below in the frozen basin at the base of the immense cliff, down there with the last of the ammunition and dwindling stores of frozen meat. He's been searching since dawn for game he hopes to shoot with the patrol's only rifle, a .30-30. Ptarmigan, marmot, ermine, a stranded moose, anything. None of them have seen any of these creatures in a string of unbearable days that now seems to stretch far out to their own individual eternities. Just finding the hint of trail that makes up this steep pass that he and Galpin find themselves on now was difficult, near miraculous. The men hope that this thread of a path leads over the mountains to the Blackstone River valley and then along Twelvemile Creek and the safety of Dawson. Perhaps a wandering hunting party of Indians will find them or a trapper. Macdonald figures that McConnell, the most skilled hunter among the men, has an outside chance at finding meat. All of the sled dogs have been killed and eaten now that food stores are exhausted. Only some tea, a little tobacco and a few of pounds of flour remain. The stores of dried fish carried for the dogs were depleted days ago.

Macdonald hooks his arms beneath Galpin's armpits, the man too exhausted to move himself. He drags him inches at a time farther behind a jumble of rocks that provides some relief from the screaming wind. After what seems hours he accomplishes his goal, out of breath, mad from hunger, and nearly insane from loneliness. He positions Galpin against the base of a round boulder. The man mutters "Thank you, Sir. I'll have more strength tomorrow," then closes his eyes. Galpin's feet point down to the valley far below like a human compass searching for the direction home. His arms are crossed upon his chest as though he is in deep thought while in corpse-like repose.

Macdonald pulls his remaining blanket from around his shoulders, rips the tattered wool in half and covers the other man. Galpin rouses himself once more and looks up at the Inspector, who retrieves a ragged, scorched handkerchief from a pocket and wraps it carefully around his companion's neck.

"We'll see this one through, Sir," said Galpin. "We've had worse scrapes before in this god-forsaken country. No winter blow will do us in."

"Good man, Corporal," said Macdonald with a forced smile. The two have indeed been through hard times, but as tough as this trip has become? The Inspector doubts this, but retains an attitude of confidence in the surety of the men's survival. Perhaps this confidence is born from desperation caused by extreme privation, the brutal cold. "I'm sorry that we'll not see this patrol through in better condition, but we do what we must. We'll be in headquarters at Dawson City in front of a roaring fire drinking whiskey before long. Count on that. "

Macdonald turns away from Galpin and faces the gale. He screams in anger and misery, the effort sending pain ripping through his frost-burned lungs. He looks back down the wicked path they've crawled up and yells "How far? How far?" He looks over to Galpin and whispers through cracked and blackened lips "We're not finished, yet." The man doesn't hear the words. He's drifted off within his own mind. Macdonald pulls himself closer to Galpin. He settles into a sitting position, knees pulled to his chest. and sheds his fur-lined mittens. He stretches what remains of his bare hands, long emaciated fingers extended out, over an imaginary fire. He works those hands together over this flaming illusion as though he's conducting a flickering orchestra and begins to feel the warmth that comes from a life beyond desperation, a place where the body barely lives in this world, where the soul is already preparing to rise to a calmer realm.

Theirs is a trip other men had made before them, six times between 1904-1910. The others had set out in winter like he had bound for Dawson City nearly 500 miles to south to deliver reports, dispatches and mail. Or in the opposite direction beginning in Dawson and bound for McPherson. They'd all made the arduous trek successfully, sometimes cold, hungry and frostbitten, but they'd made the run. Those patrols completed their missions and then those men were able to enjoy the warmth, food and amenities that the gold rush city of Dawson or the outpost had to offer. But Macdonald's patrol is different. Everything seems to go from chaotic to worse. The Inspector, who is a skilled far north campaigner, is unable to understand the nature of his failure nor is he able to accept his possible fate. He leans closer to the fire burning in his mind, one that seems to shimmer and sparkle warmly before him. He says to those dancing flames "Where did I go wrong? Where?"

~ ~ ~

Life is anything but cold or barren on this sunny, September afternoon in 1910. The cold of winter is nearby, but for now remains stationary over the polar ice cap, though a sudden shift in barometric pressure will send the first frigid blast of the season south over the land. The Peel River slices through the heart of this part of the far north country as it winds its way northeast from the rugged mountains in the Yukon that are the stream's remote headwaters. The river then plummets through deep canyons until the current flattens out along a broad alluvial valley and flows on through the Northwest Territories past Fort McPherson well above the Arctic Circle, finally merging with the enormous Mackenzie, a river miles wide and over fifty feet deep in places. The Peel is a brisk ride through wild paradise – tundra, brush, birch and pine trees and mosses are glowing with an intense autumn radiance that flares briefly before the onset of the long, dark winter. Purples, oranges, crimsons, yellows, every color imaginable, shimmer beneath an intense sun and a clear royal blue sky. The air smells of approaching cold, the moving water and the trees.

Moose stand shoulder deep in lakes and ponds munching aquatic plants, huge masses of green vegetation hanging from their jaws, water streaming down. Grizzly bears forage on nearby slopes in a late-season frenzy, the large animals crashing through the willow and alder. The bears devour berries, leaves and stems. They aren't discriminate. There is no time for such luxuries. Grayling slash and leap along the water's surface chasing rising insects. The fish have evolved over hundreds of thousands of years swimming in the ice-cold waters that tumbled and crashed at the bases of the mile-high or more ice sheets that covered much of North America periodically until about 10,000 years ago when the ice retreated leaving the rivers and mountains of this autumn day. They have learned to survive in this unforgiving environment. Eventually the walls of ice will return. Life will be forced to move south into more and more cramped quarters, but the grayling will survive in this fierce, fluctuating boundary between ice and green land.

The Peel rushes and glides to its own rhythms, drifting beneath overhanging pines, along a streambed of colorful, boulders, rock and gravel its surface smooth, calm, mirror like. Stark mountains rise in all directions. Dark green stands of pines cover the lower slopes, but a thousand feet above the valley floor the sharp ridges and wide cirques are treeless, the only vegetation is sparse flecks of shrubs and mosses that flicker in wavering intensities as a light band of clouds plays with the sun. Intense shafts of light dance over the purple-gray and orange-pink layers of rock that form the upper levels of the peaks.

Fort McPherson is located on a high bank along the east side of the Peel River, named after the former Prime Minister of Great Britain John Peel. The post sits on a mostly dry expanse of land within the tundra. By the time the river has wandered this far north it's become a wide, brown-colored flow filled with the rich soils absorbed as it sailed beneath thick stands of pine and birch. The post was established to police the area's fur trade and traders, many of whom were less than scrupulous individuals, and to try and keep a lid on the violence often associated with mining claim disputes that arise on a regular basis along the placer gold operations in the surrounding mountain drainages. The post was originally establish for trade in 1840 by the Hudson Bay Company and named after one of its most intrepid traders, Murdoch McPherson. The Indian name is a more lyrical, *Teel'lit Zhen* or "head of the waters."

There are times when this is a fantastic place. Fantastic in the sense of perpetual day or never-ending night; or fantastic as herds of thousands upon thousands of caribou make their way south each fall from near the Arctic Ocean down hundreds of miles to the tundra and relative shelter of the Blackstone River Plateau. Or fantastic when moose and grizzly wander through the post ravaging dumps, mauling huskies and tearing doors off their sturdy iron hinges as the animals follow their noses scrounging for food stored inside the rough-hewn log or thick wood plank structures. Sometimes the great bears appear with the only apparent intent of causing mayhem, venting natural rages or just raising hell because they can. Thick layers of fur and fat make the grizzlies nearly impervious to the rifle shots from traders and Mounties. The sole result of these efforts normally being to further anger the bears that then proceed to smash, claw and bludgeon any object or creature in their way. While Fort McPherson's inhabitants are familiar with this violence, they've never gotten used to it. Merely one more difficulty to contend with in the North.

The nearest posts to McPherson are at Herschel Island just a few miles off the mainland in the Beufort Sea. The outpost, established at this northernmost of all continental whaling ports, is a couple of hundred difficult miles away along a vague trail that is only passable, and this just barely, when the muskeg swamps, marshy lakes and ponds along with the rivers and creeks freeze for the winter offering a fairly safe travel corridor; and Fort Good Hope located 284 miles up the Mackenzie on the rivers eastern side.

The 200-foot-high bank fronting the river at McPherson makes the hauling of supplies from a supply boat an arduous task. Goods are ferried to shore in rowboats, then hauled by the men in crude packs or in wooden crates up the steep, loose-soiled incline to either the Hudson Bay warehouse or the NWMP storage facilities. This is sweaty, muscle-burning, mosquito-ridden labor, a simple task of a couple hours often takes most of a full summer's day or is nearly impossible following a rainstorm. Despite this difficulty, McPherson sits atop the driest, most conveniently located place for miles around.

Limitless tracts of swamp and numerous lakes dot the terrain farther east of camp. Because of this, during the brief summer months, hordes of mosquitoes make life miserable for man, sled dog and wild animal alike. There is no escaping the blood-seeking insects that swarm in clouds that will at times literally blot out the sun. The noisome creatures find their way into the eyes, ears, mouths, through thick clothing and hide, and into the rough buildings of the settlement. Breathing becomes a chore as taking the shallowest of breaths often sucks in a dozen mosquitoes. Faces and hands become swollen from the bites and the scratching attempts to alleviate the maddening itching that accompanies the inflammation. The Indians are immune from most of the effects of these bites after generations of exposure. One day last month a trapper fell drunkenly unconscious in the marshy land behind the Hudson Bay store. He never woke up. His desiccated body was discovered next morning. Mosquitoes had sucked the blood out of him as they have been known to do to caribou. The insects often drive these creatures mad and into a stampede that lasts for hours as the caribou vainly attempt to flee the pests. The hum of the billions of mosquitoes along with a healthy population of black flies is as constant from June through early August as is the sun that never drops below the horizon at this time of the year.

Fort McPherson is more than fifty miles above the Arctic Circle in the Northwest Territories. Days of twenty-four hours of sunlight turn life into a surreal dance where morning might as well be midnight and the reverse holds true as well. Because of this, the members of the Royal Northwest Mounted Police stationed here try to adhere to a regime of rising at 5 a.m., if they aren't already awake in the broad daylight, and proceed with the day's duties until 5 p.m. Mess is at 7 p.m. and normally consists of dried or smoked Arctic char or Dolly Vardon taken from the Peel or fresh moose made into a mulligan stew or caribou along with strong tea and occasionally vegetables grown in the post's garden; or in lean times, pemmican, a mixture of pounded meat, fat and wild berries. Lights out, something of a running joke among the men in the summer months, is at eleven. All of this is as flexible as the weather is variable. Sudden rain or snow squalls packing winds near 100 mph can build up over the northern horizon then whip down on the fort in less than an hour. Hail and sleet can knock a man out and slice exposed skin in an instant. The buildings usually survive the onslaught; and the harsh weather wipes the air clean of bugs for an hour or two. Blessed relief.

Loucheux Indians arrive at all hours of the day bringing furs – marten, mink, white fox, wolverine, wolf, otter, weasel, beaver, lynx and muskrat – they've acquired from trapping, dried fish, moose or caribou. They camp in makeshift tent-like structures that resemble the gers of their Mongolian ancestors. The people themselves feature the dark skin, high cheekbones and piercing eyes of their fierce brethren. Those of their band who spend more time at the fort have constructed cabins that resemble downsized, flimsier versions of the white man's structures. These are adorned on the outside with moose and caribou racks, piles of bones from these animals, and woven-grass rugs covering the dirt floors.

Trappers – French, English, Scottish, Canadian, American – work their way up from the Mackenzie River whose junction with the Peel lay thirty miles to the north or drift down on the rapid current of the Peel and its tributaries, like the rushing Porcupine, Hart or Wind, bringing in often enormous loads of furs from the little explored Wernecke, Knorr and Bonnet Plume Ranges.

In 1903 Fort McPherson was, even by northern standards, a tumbledown, ramshackle situation that included five Hudson Bay buildings. The leavings of dozens of sled dogs were piled everywhere. The two exceptions were the church and missionary house, structures kept in good repair by an Anglican Archdeacon who not only exposed the Loucheux to his religion, but also taught many of them to read, write and speak English. Many of the Indians were far more conversant in the language than the white trappers. By this fall of 1910 all of the structures had been renovated, and several of them enlarged with glass windows added. The Mountie headquarters now include a dining room, billiard parlor – both with fine woven wool carpets from Morocco. A touch of the ostentatious life here in the wilderness. And there are new barracks plus boarding facilities for the many sled dogs that passed their days sleeping, growling, fighting among themselves or barking in a riotous chorus that raucously competes with the mosquitoes. The residue of the dogs is now cleaned up on a weekly basis and deposited well behind the kennels in a compost pile that eventually fertilizes a garden that produces a surprising abundance, considering the short growing season, of large tomatoes, peas, potatoes and maze. The Hudson Bay Company's structures have all been improved and weatherproofed. Bales of furs purchased from trappers and Indians are stacked along the south wall of the Company's main building as high as the roofline. Low-lying areas of water within the town site had been filled in, slightly alleviating the bug infestation.

The Loucheux are constant residents of the fort if only on a nomadic basis as they come and go in subtle syncopation with ancient hunting seasons and, to some extent, as their free-roaming nature dictates. They are native Athabascans who've hunted, trapped and fished the upper Peel for centuries. They are a generally friendly band of aboriginal people who prefer helping those in need, even outsiders such as the posted Mounties, to fighting or quarrelling. The whites called these indigenous people *Kutchin,* which means "people from a distant place." Conversely, the word means "white people" to the Indians. The French voyageurs of the early 1800s applied the term Loucheux to all aboriginal people of the northern Yukon, the word translating to "slant-eyed" in French. Despite the obvious differences in culture and appearance, a relationship bordering on symbiotic established itself among the fort's inhabitants. The Loucheux guide the whites into and out of remote uncharted land showing them where and how to trap the game that abounds in the area during the warmer months of the year. In return they receive payment in the form of goods that include flour, tobacco, firearms and ammunition. Fights among all of the inhabitants are few and problems with liquor are rare. The penalties for trading whiskey to the Indians are severe. Often lengthy incarceration or banishment from the region. Intoxicated Loucheux often spend several weeks in the small jail as punishment.

Following their evening meal, Constables R.G. McConnell and George Fraser stroll from headquarters towards the wooden-planked overlook that offered an expansive view of the river for many miles both north and south. Muskeg and diminutive spruce trees that grow at odd angles resembling drunks staggering from a Dawson City saloon stretch off in limitless distance. Several ravens are strutting along the far shore, the enormous birds pecking and squawking as they search for dead fish and other detritus. The men, both in their mid-twenties and both sporting thick, though well-trimmed, mustaches, light their pipes filling the air around them with thick clouds of rich smoke. They each carry a cup of Darjeeling tea that they sip between puffs on the burning Connemara Virginia Blend, uncommon luxuries delivered on the last supply boat a month ago. The two Mounties allow themselves these slight indulgencies each evening when they scan the horizon and discuss the day's events along with future plans and tasks. If a person didn't know better, he would quite naturally assume that the two men are brothers or at the very least, first cousins. Both are a couple of inches short of six feet tall. Both weigh about one-sixty-five pounds and both have thick heads of dark red hair and flaming mustaches to match. Their voices are neither deep nor high pitched, but somewhere in between with a trace of the Scottish Highlands' burr working around the edges of their speech.

Several hard frosts, expected this late in August, have blanketed the countryside in the past week eliminating the last of the mosquitoes and black flies. Moving about outdoors without perpetually batting and cursing the insects is a blessed relief and a joy.

"Damn nice to be without the buggers," said McConnell.

"Indeed. I feel as though I've been set free not having to battle those things," said Fraser. "Reminds me of when the cold hits the highlands back home and the mosquitoes die out for the year. And the ground cover turns those intense shades of red, orange and purple. Loch Leven trout run in a burn near our home, too. Fine fishing. Miss that, though the char and Dollys in this river make up for it some."

"The tundra in this land does indeed color up in ways that remind me of that country," said McConnell. "Hard not to miss family and home when the weather and the land here conspire to remind me of Scotland. No rivers like this Peel, though, or the Mackenzie. God, this is enormous country. But once again it's the time when the days are visibly growing shorter. We're losing nearly seven minutes of light per day. Soon it will be a dozen."

McConnell turns to the sun that is still well above the horizon at 8:30, though it clearly appears to be swinging to the south.

Both men are from the Scottish Highlands, growing up only a few miles apart on a high plateau of heather and moss riddled with lakes and streams that formed in the mountains of the interior. Each also has family in the North Sea port of Wick, where family members have toiled in the shipyards for generations. Each man came over with their immediate families when they traveled by steamer to Halifax in search of more prosperous lives working as ship builders at one of the many yards in that Nova Scotia harbor. The pair finished schooling in the port city and then enlisted in the Royal Canadian Mounted Police. Their lives parallel and mirror each other. When the two were posted to the recruit school in Regina during the spring of 1907 within weeks of each other, the event came as no surprise to either of them. They'd talked about just such a happenstance so often, that when they'd received their orders it was as though some minor master plan were being set in motion. One that was eagerly anticipated and expected. While they learned the ropes of life in the RNWMP, they also enjoyed their free time in the rough and tumble city that seemed to be a mixture of equal parts of the wild west, the prairie and the northland trapper lifestyle. In town they learned to drink whiskey without showing the liquor's effects, avoid trouble with subtle diplomacy and also to read people – their expressions, movements – all slight tells to inner motivations, cons and angles.

Yet, despite all this adventure and the new way of life, the lure of the Canadian west and ultimately the far North dominated their thoughts.

Seven months later two openings appeared at Fort McPherson in the Northwest Territories as the Royal Northwest Mounted Police pushed ahead in not only maintaining but strengthening its presence in the remote northern Canadian territories. McConnell and Fraser immediately applied for the positions and because of their excellent records during the past year in Saskatchewan, they soon found themselves traveling by dog sled across the frozen Canadian prairie in early March. They moved through the lengthening periods of daylight across the vast distances of the snow-covered northern high plains, landscape that become hypnotic in its white featurelessness as it gradually shifted to boreal forest the farther north they went. There were thousands of square miles of virgin forest growing silently in the now-frozen muskeg swamp that rolled on like a still-life sea, apparently without end. The dogs pulled them along corridors of frozen rivers and lakes where they spotted an occasional Meti hunting party, French/Indians relocated from their Red River homeland in northern Manitoba far to the east, seeking moose holding in the dense bush. Bells attached to the leather traces tinkled in the chill air. They sighted wolves ghosting along shorelines casting quick, nervous glances behind them at the passing sleds. And twice they spotted wolverines, each one snarling and charging the sleds as they glided through the powdery snow, runners hissing softly in the stillness. They also passed by groups of woodland bison, the enormous, humped beasts scarcely noticing their passage, clouds of steam rising from their black snouts, yearlings huddle in the middle of the animals for warmth.

Mile after mile they traveled with two other Mounties, both of whom had long careers under their belts and were now inspectors. The older men had made this run to Fort Chipewyan on the Slave River in the far Northeastern corner of Alberta and were in charge of the trip. After resting and restocking their provisions, the men raced down the river to Fort Resolution on Great Slave Lake. As they neared the settlement they encountered increasing numbers of Indians that were members of the Slavey band of the Dene, aboriginals migrated over the now submerged Bering land bridge on their way from Mongolia to this country thousands of years ago.

They waited here for spring breakup in late-May passing the time hunting and learning all they could from veteran Mounties about this immense, intimidating country and the land where they were bound. Things like what plants provided nourishment and when they were edible and where they were found; how to build lean-to shelters in a hurry for warmth and shelter from thunderstorms that rose above the horizon in minutes; how to build fires without matches; and some Dene language.

They heard tales of men lost in the trackless bush in the dead of winter, out of food. Starving men that were driven to kill and eat their sled dogs, then after this meat was consumed, they boiled and ate the leather harnesses and traces. Finally weakened to the point of death, these men

15

sometimes fell upon each other, killing for the meat that remained on bodies that resembled skeletons or they ate the remains of corpses that froze solid in the deadly cold night. The two were told this as though the stories were myth or distant legend and not the actions of sane, decent men, but the message was clear – the North is an unforgiving, brutal land that drives men to unspeakable acts in the name of survival. McConnell and Fraser glanced at each other, their eyes transmitting the mutual message "Not us. Not ever."

After weeks of impatient waiting, the two finally shipped out one early-June dawn by steamer across the enormous body of water and then down hundreds of miles on the Mackenzie River to the mouth of the Peel where they took a smaller riverboat upstream to Fort McPherson. The trip across Great Slave was an adventure as one angry storm after another threatened to sink the ship called The Firth. Waves of thirty feet lashed them on this inland sea. Constant gales packing sleet, rain, snow and hail hammered the vessel. The experienced captain stayed well away from the dangerous reefs that made the southern shoreline hazardous, one that had claimed dozens of craft in recent years. Despite icy fog he managed to keep the ship out in the open where it could ride out the storms, riding into each series of waves with a steady, heavyweight surety that came from a hull design meant for the unforgiving North Sea blows common to the builders' British Isle home waters.

Eventually they reached the lake's outlet where the Mackenzie was several miles wide as it flowed past Fort Providence. Both McConnell and Fraser were accustomed to the much smaller rivers of Scotland and lately those that wandered the plains of Saskatchewan. Here those rivers would be considered creeks and more than likely remained unnamed on the few rough maps that charted the area. The scale of the country was so much larger than either of them had ever experienced that putting any of what they saw into perspective, into a juxtaposition with their former lives, was a dizzying, difficult process. Months were needed before they would be able to assimilate the power, energy and little-known majesty of the North, let alone the geography of country so large the provinces of Alberta and British Columbia could be contained there in with room for the states of Montana and Wyoming left over.

The Mackenzie rolled northward towards the high Arctic passing beneath enormous bluffs and banks that appeared as earthen ramparts to the travelers. To the west range after range of mountains, each one higher and more jagged than the next with snow and ice crowned peaks that tore at the blue sky, ran on forever. In the south Nahanni Butte marked the beginning of still more wild and unexplored country, the geologic structures resembling island mountains shimmered softly blue nearly 100 miles distant. Along the eastern shore the Ebbets Hills, and the McConnell and Franklin Mountains defined that horizon, the bare, rounded rock summits rolling off beyond the horizon. Game was everywhere – moose fording tributary creeks and rivers, bison standing on top of the bluffs, marten and snowshoe hare scampering along banks next to running water. Huge fish leaped from the surface of the river constantly – northern pike, grayling, Dolly Vardon, iconnu – crashing back through the surface in a crescendo of spray that reflected the sun's light in hot prismatic radiance. Geese and ducks moved north in flocks of uncountable numbers, their cries and honkings overcoming the ship engine's steady drown. Eagles rode thermals far above them, circling, always circling until they were lost from view.

"I've never seen anything like this," said Fraser as he tamped more tobacco in his pipe. "The land never ends. There's so much of it. And the animals. A man would have to work to starve in this country."

17

"I agree. I'm overwhelmed. It's too much for the mind to absorb all at once. Such abundance and life," said McConnell. "And the sky, it's shade of blue and the layers of cloud are new to me, almost unreal. But I wonder what this land is like in winter when it's well below zero and the wind howls down on us from the North Pole. Is there game about then or do we hang on and pray we don't starve? Those tales of men going mad and eating each other in those mountains haunt me. I can't imagine being that hungry. I think that I would prefer to starve to death."

The two went silent and the Firth cruised easily downriver pushed along by the heavy current of spring runoff.

Eventually they reached the river's confluence with the Peel where they transferred their gear, supplies of tea, ammunition, cornmeal, tobacco and several bags of mail and dispatches to a 22-foot canoe manned by a white who called himself Twelve-foot Davis and several Loucheaux, including one who seemed to think everything was funny, a wide semi-toothless grin a constant feature on his face as were eyes that sparkled and seemed to dance over all they saw. All this was constantly punctuated by an ever-present, deep-voiced chuckle of "Uh hum, uh hum, uh hum." His name was Njootli and the others seemed to take orders from him as though this native jester knew secrets the rest could only guess at. The twenty-plus-mile trip against the current took two days as the river wound through lowlands of muskeg and dwarf spruce and willow. Mosquitoes were beginning to hatch in great numbers as the days grew longer and warmer. They caused great discomfort to the three white men, who spent as much time killing the insects as they did anything else. The Loucheaux appeared not to notice the winged antagonists. McConnell and Fraser slept little that night on the river, instead passing the hours stoking a bonfire that they coaxed into producing dense clouds of smoke by covering it with pine boughs they soaked in river water. This had little effect on the mosquitoes, but helped occupy the two men. Njootli thought this was hilarious. He'd point at the two of them stooped over the fire immersed in the choking clouds, then make buzzing sounds like the bugs before booming forth "Uh hum, uh hum." The newcomers found nothing funny about their itching misery or Njootli. Their assessment of the man would change over time.

When they reached the landing at Fort McPherson they leaped from the canoe and dragged their belongings up the switchback trail climbing up the bank as quickly as possible, slipping and sliding back down towards the river in their careless haste. "Uh hum, uh hum" followed their every step.

Over the following three years the men became skilled Arctic wilderness inhabitants, earning hard-won reputations as competent, prudent individuals. Men you could trust with your life. In the middle of a winter blizzard, during an all-out hatch of mosquitoes and black flies, or at the height of spring runoff when melting snow and ice from the surrounding mountain ranges turned creeks into raging torrents and rivers like the Peel into swirling maelstroms choked with downed trees, McConnell and Fraser are now counted on to provide level-headed advice and swift, stern but fair action for whatever problems arose. Whether it was sunken canoes, lost sled dogs, claim jumping, whiskey-fueled arguments, it didn't matter, they handle each situation or disaster with calm dispatch. Few ever dispute their decisions or the justice they mete out. Even Njootli, who is now a permanent resident of the fort, will accompany one or both of the men when they travel far into the mountains to check out reports on plundered trap lines or injured prospectors or conflicts between the Louchcaux or Dene or Inuits or the whites or any combination of the four.

"You two start out as green as the moss in spring, but now you know enough not to kill yourselves in those mountains, uh hum, uh hum," said Njootli one day as he pointed to the distant foothills of the Canyon Ranges that stretched their timbered feet northward towards the muskeg vastness that reaches all the way to Mackenzie Bay and the Beaufort Sea. There are times when the wind is out of the north that a person can smell, imagine that he can taste, the salt of the sea. "I go with you damn near everywhere, even in winter, maybe. Maybe. That season can be cold death to those with little respect for the land and its spirits."

Both McConnell and Fraser took this as high praise from a man known from Herschel Island to Fort Selkirk on the Yukon River as the finest tracker and woodsman in the North. The two are now in charge of the post including the three other junior Constables that make up the McPherson contingent.

When Inspector Wallams Macdonald stopped at the fort on his way to a posting at Herschel Island in late-summer of 1908, he was impressed with the attention to duty and detail, the enthusiasm, and candor that the younger men displayed. The junior Mounties all went about their daily tasks without being supervised. Work was accomplished in an orderly fashion. Morale was good as Macdonald observed all of the men helping each other and joking among themselves. One of his orders was to assess how things were going at Fort McPherson and to make any changes he deemed necessary. The only improvement Macdonald directed was moving the community dump from near the kennels to a slight rise outside of town that was drier and down wind from the prevailing breezes. He pointed out that a low, stockade-type fence around the refuse pile would help keep out scavengers. When McConnell commented that he couldn't for the life of him figure out why he hadn't thought of this, the Inspector, with a dry hint of humor in his voice said, "Sometimes the obvious is the most frequently overlooked."

Upon the next batch of dispatches Macdonald sent along on the 1908-09 winter mail run from Herschel Island by way of Fort McPherson to Dawson City, a distance of more than 700 miles, he informed Superintendent Trevor Finlay at Division Headquarters that he had left the pair in charge of running the operation in the region and requested an increase in pay for the men with the recommendation that they both be promoted to the rank of corporal by the summer of 1911. Information and orders move slowly in this country. In yearly increments that progress as do the seasons, mainly during the cold months from mid-November when the land and rivers are ice-over, frozen solid through mid-April before ice-out. More high praise from still another consummate north country voyager.

"Those damned ravens have beaks large enough to hack through our barracks," said Fraser. The sun is now barely above the western horizon, its light shading from yellow to a golden orange that lights the land with an otherworldly radiance. The downscale spruce and the banks of the Peel cast lengthy deep purple shadows that stretch across the tundra like slender, lengthening fingers. All is quiet save for the near subliminal purlings of the river's current and an occasional squawk from the birds. "They're a bit of a nuisance, but the place would feel empty, like a vital piece is missing, if they were to leave."

"I agree. Smart birds they are, too," said McConnell. "I watched two of them work open the lid on the lard bin the other day. One wedged its beak between lid and rim, then the other widened the gap before both of them flipped it onto the ground. Wish some of our dogs had their smarts. Seems like mostly they fight each other and conspire to tangle their traces, all except Wraithmolian."

The dog is a mix of husky and Irish Wolfhound that has produced a creature over 160 pounds that is deep-chested and long-legged with enormous paws that seem to ride across the surface of deep powdery snow like webbed snowshoes. This dog, Wraithmolian Gonne, is named after his father, an Irish national champion – Wraithmolian of Tarkin. His mother, also a national champion, is called Maude Mad Gonne. The brindled animal cuts a striking figure with its enormous, square-jawed head and long rough fur that also features the dense cream guard hairs of the husky breed. Sometimes when wolves howl in the night, the hound will answer with a deep, primordial bellow that thunders in the darkness, often silencing the wolves, who may wonder if their ultimate leader is now present in this mysterious landscape.

"That one's a fine one. A real leader," said Fraser.

"Perhaps that's what Conan Doyle had in mind when he wrote *The Hound of the Baskervilles,*" said McConnell.

The talk turns to an evacuation they made last week of a prospector who'd sliced his foot from the webbing between his big toe and adjacent digit while drunkenly attempting to split wood. Word of the injury reached them by way of a wandering Loucheaux hunting party that encountered the man while on its way north to the Mackenzie Delta. When the Mounties found him, his foot had gone to gangrene and McConnell was forced to hack the foot away below the shin with his large knife that had a serrated edge near the handle. He completed the ugly task while Fraser held the screaming man as steady as possible. Ugly, but necessary, work. The two Mounties then built a travois of spruce trunks and hauled the man back to the post, more than forty miles by lashing the thing to there shoulders and chests. McConnell and Fraser bushwhacked through the dense forest and swampland without sleep or even periods of rest, drinking water and chewing chunks of bannock, a dry, unleavened bread made from barley flour, as they struggled back to the post. The trip took thirty hours and the feat already making the isolated rounds of the region. Another legend brewing beneath the Arctic sky.

"Lord in heaven I hated that, but we were given no choice," said McConnell. "I could smell the rotting flesh a hundred yards away as we came up Shatlah Creek. For once I'm glad for the whiskey. Delirious he was and unconscious we rendered him with the last of that keg. Still, his pain was enormous."

"One of Njootli's wives is caring for him. Even carved him a crutch and is fashioning a cap out of tanned moose hide for his stump," said Fraser. "Njootli said he'd be on his feet, the bugger launched a few 'Uh hums' at that little pun, in another week or so. He even offered the man that wife, saying that "a man's serious greedy" if he has more than four. That Loucheaux is like the ravens. The place wouldn't be the same without any of them."

The pair laughs through clouds of the smoldering Connemara tobacco smoke they expel and they sip the now-cool tea. Next the two discuss the letter that arrived from Inspector Macdonald earlier today from Herschel Island.

The missive was carried by a trapper named Louis Cardinal, a man who invested more than thirty years in the Canadian Arctic. Never to be rich or famous, he is a man of few wants, a man who desires only the freedom to move about as whim dictates and to live this vagabond existence alone. Up until a few years ago he had trapped and prospected for rare gems – rubies and emeralds he claimed – in the upper reaches of the South Nahanni River in a place known as Deadmen's Basin. Rumors of a rich find by Cardinal had made the rounds from post to post, but if this is indeed the case, the fifty-year-old recluse is not letting on.

When asked about this he shrugs and says "I don't think so. I'm too damn busy trapping the furs and shooting at the grizzly bear." And that is that. He will utter this brief comment and then walk away.

When two other trappers moved in twenty miles down river, Cardinal decided that things were too crowded so he traveled over many miles of unmapped and probably never visited mountains, eventually settling on a severe valley east of the Bonnet Plume Range 100 miles south of Fort McPherson. He only comes out of that wild country to trade furs, sell gold dust and some large nuggets at the current rate of exchange; and a couple of times to make a trip to Herschel when he hears that the whaling ships are in. Sailors make easy pickings when it comes to obtaining top dollar for his furs that are some of the thickest, richest ever seen in Arctic Circle country. He has spent the past couple of weeks at the port trading his furs with members of the vessels' crews.

His task complete, furs sold at a handsome profit, Cardinal began the 260-mile journey by striking out from the barren grounds of Herschel Island heading directly across the several miles of calm open water. He then kept his 18-foot canoe tight to the shore of Mackenzie Bay dodging sudden squalls by sliding into sheltered inlets and camping for the night if necessary.

On the second day Cardinal spotted an enormous, they all seem enormous when a man is alone in this country, polar bear that picked up the man's scent from an on-shore breeze and proceeded to track him for many miles both by loping along the rocky shoreline and by swimming at a steady distance behind him for hours with no apparent signs of growing tired. Cardinal wouldn't provide that much food for the bear, but polar bears were known for their tenacity concerning the hunting of prey regardless of its size.

The bear's never-ending hunt began to wear on Cardinal, who was fully aware of the mean disposition of polar bears and their deserved reputation as both man killers and man-eaters. The trapper finally pushed hard to a rock outcropping in a small bay on the inside of Tent Island near the Mackenzie Delta. Quickly beaching and securing his canoe, Cardinal climbed a rise to a promising vantage point looking out over the water and waited for the bear. The animal came paddling towards him at a surprising speed, its large paws churning the sapphire water to a bubbling white froth wake. Cardinal sighted in with his .303 Martini-Metford rifle and fired five times, aiming just behind the bear's neck. He heard all five shots strike their target with a solid, though muffled, "whumpf." The great bear thrashed and tumbled in the shallow water struggled to shore where it rose on its hind legs, standing ten feet tall, roaring in pain and rage. It then dropped down on all fours and charged Cardinal's position, bellowing as it came with freight train intensity, bloody froth streaming from its open jaws. He looked through his sights once again and could see the killing anger lighting the polar bear's eyes with a yellow glow. Cardinal fired four of the remaining five rounds in the ten-shot magazine at the slightly exposed chest and head on the onrushing animal, each bullet hitting its mark, one shot ricocheted off the bear's thick skull and caromed into a jumble of boulders. The bear halted in its tracks, front legs buckling, head crashing to the ground. Then the creature rose on its hind legs once more. The bear roared in dying madness and crumpled in a heap on the cold, cobbled rock beach. The trapper approached cautiously and fired the last round in the clip into the animal's ear making sure it was dead.

Cardinal spent the next several hours skinning the bear. He scraped as much clinging flesh from the green hide as he could at the wet, chilled location before spreading a light layer of coarse salt on the skin. He then rolled up the dirty and bloody white fur and struggled to load its bulky weight, over two hundred pounds, in the center of his canoe. Next he pushed off and began working the heavily laden and now sluggish canoe through the labyrinthine maze of islands and channels that make up the thousands of square miles of delta country. After several days paddling against the languid current of the braided Mackenzie, he eventually located the relatively straightforward Husky Channel on the western edge of the delta, a corridor that led to the Peel and Fort McPherson, one that was used frequently by aboriginals and whites alike over the years.

When the Macdonald message arrived, McConnell was out working with the three other Constables repairing a stretch of road that wound towards a traditional fall camp of the Inuits, a place where the Indians dried the spawning Arctic char that moved up the Peel from the Arctic Ocean each fall beginning in late August. The fish are often over twenty pounds, hard and bright silver from their months in the sea. Within a few days of swimming in the freshwater of the Peel the males' backs become humped, jaws extended and hooked, and their colors changed to bronze-orange along the back shifting to indigo along flanks with crimson bellies spattered with blood-red spotting throughout. A riotous, magnificent example of Arctic splendor. The flesh is hot orange and delicately sweet when smoked or dried, rich in protein and vitamin E. The Inuits will put away literally tons of char each autumn in their annual ritual of preparing for the hardships of winter. The road is often underwater and the spruce logs used to make the passage at least a hopeful possibility are rot and break constantly. These need to be replaced so that the Indians can haul the fish pulled from their nets stretched out in eddies and pools up and down the Peel up to their encampment, where drying racks and fire pits have stood for many years. Here they prepare the filleted flesh of the char.

Before the construction of Fort McPherson, the Inuits

had hauled their catch directly through what is now the center of the post. For years now they've had to detour around the northern edge of the fort. McConnell and Fraser, in an attempt at establishing good will among the Indians and making life a bit easier for them, designed a road that lead more or less directly to the site, one that passed the northern edge of the fort. They completed this project during their first fall in the area. Maintaining and improving the road had become something of an obsession for the two Mounties, one both the Inuits and Loucheaux appreciated and also found fascinating, this constant attention to a pathway that shifts and heaves with each hard frost or is washed partially away each spring or during severe storms. The Indians being wanderers who move as they wished, as conditions dictate, are unable to fathom this ongoing attempt at permanence in an ever-changing land.

When the exhausted Cardinal hand-delivered the message, Fraser thanked him and poured the trapper a large measure of rum into a coffee cup. The grateful Cardinal downed the drink in one take and tottered off to the Hudson Bay barracks for a long rest. Fraser then tore open the envelope.

For NWMP Constables McConnell and Fraser -"Will leave Herschel on 10th November 1910. Expect to arrive at Fort McPherson by 15th November. Begin making arrangements for dogs, equipment, provisions so that all is near ready when I arrive. Attempt to engage Loucheaux guide known as Njootli at standard rate (negotiable) for trip.
Inspector Wallams Macdonald, R.N.W.M.P., 25th August 1910

"According to the letter, Macdonald should be here by the middle of November at the latest if all goes well," said

Fraser as he relights his pipe with a stick match. "That will give us plenty of time to prepare for the run to Dawson. Njootli hasn't said whether he'll be our guide or not. Can't think of a better man to find the way over the pass. He navigates as if he has an internal compass or natural intuitiveness. It's spooky at times. Tricky country along the Wernecke Mountains. Those two trappers, Johnson and LeBarge, almost froze to death last winter before they picked up the trail through the cut in those mountains and down the Blackstone. Windy as hell up there, too. Seems to build up in the Canyon Ranges then whoosh through the gap like water from a burst dam. Getting lost in that country is not good business."

"Don't worry George. If Njootli quits the show, Macdonald says he can count on Galpin. He's made the run before," said McConnell. "If we strike out around the twentieth of December we should be having dinner and drinks at The Columbian Chop House in Dawson by January 15th. A warm fire, good food, single malt scotch, a soft bed with linen sheets. That will be a fine end to a cold journey."

"Maybe the Inspector believes in Galpin, but Njootli says the country from here to there looks completely different when a man runs it from north to south the first time rather than the opposite way," said Fraser. "He said that going one way hardly gives a man experience coming back. In fact, he said that if enough time has passed between trips, the previous runs can confuse a man, 'dance trickery in his mind' is the way Njootli put things. That man will hold to preconceived notions gained from the other trips and not pay attention to either his compass or common sense. Orders are orders, so there's no questioning my resolve or commitment, but I'd feel better if that crazy Indian came along for the ride."

"I agree, but we'll mange, especially with Wraith in the

lead of the first sled. Here, I see you're out. Have some of my tobacco," said McConnell offering his leather pouch, one he'd received from Njootli, whose first wife made it from a wolverine skin. The rowdy animal caught itself in a trap set near the dump outside of the fort. One of the young Constables heard its yowling and watched as the wolverine began chewing its leg bone above the foot in a desperate attempt to escape. The Mountie dispatched the animal with a single shot to the head from a .22 rifle. The hide was tanned using a paste consisting of the animal's brains, warm water and pine needles. The leather is now soft as the finest suede.

Wolverines or carcajou as the French trappers called them, are the most aggressive animals in the North Country. Indians and whites alike fear them more than polar or grizzly bears. Wolverines often weigh as much as sixty pounds. They possess razor-sharp teeth and claws and a nasty disposition. One of the animals tore down the door of the Hudson Bay storehouse and raised complete mayhem inside. All of the fort's inhabitants were awakened late one night by a guttural scream, assorted sounds of breaking glass, ripping canvas, shattering wood and puncturing tin cans. Shining a lamplight inside Mounties, Loucheaux and Company employees saw a wolverine, teeth exposed in aggression, the animal drenched in canned beans, flour, molasses and flakes of tobacco. Fraser pulled his pistol and fired three times, striking the crazed animal with each shot to no apparent effect other then its turning on the men and charging. All of them fled for the camp mess where they jammed through the entrance and bolted the door.

"This is ridiculous," said McConnell and he started to laugh. "A ground-hugging, over-grown weasel is holding the post hostage."

"Un hum, uh hum. Carcajou king of the north," said Njootli between his toothy grin.

Sounds of destruction and disaster continued for another hour and then stopped. In the light of a new day the men examined the wreckage. Perhaps a quarter of the Company's stores were destroyed as was the front door, several shelves along one wall and two windows. A trail of beans, blood and flour gradually faded as it led off across the tundra. The wolverine was never seen again. Both McConnell and Fraser wondered if the gunshots had finished the animal. Another Arctic mystery, one that only increased the infamous reputation of the carcajou.

On this late-August evening both men are dressed in crimson-colored Norfolk jackets that are the trademark of the Mounties, a clearly visible sign of authority in the north. They also have on the regulation steel gray trousers, but instead of the standard issue black Wellington boots, they each sport a pair of moose hide knee-length moccasins made for them by another one of Njootli's wives. In cold weather instead of the standard duck knee-length parka with a fur-lined collar they both wear anoraks stitched from wolf and caribou skins fur-side out and lined with the softest of beaver pelts. Filigree patterns done in gold thread decorated the fronts of both men's parkas. McConnell possesses two pairs of gloves made from wolverine skins while Fraser prefers those made from a wolf. Mukluks are fur-lined and made from the thickest of moose hides. Njootli has made several pairs of snowshoes from cured willow and birch limbs for the frames and stretched caribou rawhide for the webbing and bindings. Some are near circular ovals in shape and used for fresh powder. Others are a long, slender design for tracking through the confined spaces of the dwarf spruce and the mountain pine forests. While none of this would pass muster in Regina, in the Arctic survival is paramount, not slavish adherence to regimental dress protocol.

"I need to ask Njootli to have his first wife make me

another pair of mukluks for the trip," said Fraser. "That woman's a hellcat, but she makes the finest foot wear in all the Territories. Shall I request a pair for you? They take time and that is a commodity that runs short in a hurry without notice it always seems."

"Yes. Please do. Mukluks have become an obsession, perhaps a passion with me since that brutal cold spell two years ago, what did the mercury dip to? Seventy-two below. Cracked that fool Company clerk's teeth when he breathed directly through his mouth. Most glad he was shipped out on the spring flood. A damnable nuisance he was with his numbers and tally sheets," said McConnell. "Anyway, good mukluks are important to me as you know."

"About the only passion you've had for years up this way, eh, R.G.?"

The two men laugh at their shared isolation from women. Both of their thoughts drift to the ladies of Dawson City, both proper and professional. They smoke in silence as dusk drifts over the valley and a crescent quarter-moon rises above the mountains, it's cold silvery glow holding sufficient intensity to blot out the first early stars of the evening. In the distance wolves howl at the appearance, the lonesome cries drifting across the ground and echoing off low-rising hills in the west. Wraith is silent this evening.

A group of Lesser sandhill cranes is grouped around a wetland area not far from the fort. They clack among themselves making sounds that are far beyond ancient, as though a bunch of pterodactyls has surfaced from the Cretaceous Period for reasons known only to themselves. The birds' calls add a curious dimension to the calm evening. A small string of Tundra swans in a ragged V formation swinging down from the north, lowers and wheels overhead honking loudly among themselves, wings flared, as thcy drop down for the evening on a nearby lake. The noise of air slicing over the birds' wide wings is a deep whistle as they pass over the two men.

31

-CHAPTER TWO-

I demand that neither hardship. suffering, privation, nor fear of death should move you by a hair's breadth from carrying out your duties.

-Inspector George French
Northwest Mounted Police
1875

NEARLY A DOZEN WHALING SHIPS lie at anchor, rising slightly on the smooth water that reflects the blue sky in silver perfection. The vessels are in various states of preparation for the inactive winter months ahead. All of them are within a couple of hundred yards of the stone and pebble shoreline of Pauline Cove at Herschel Island. The bay is formed by a sweeping curve of low-lying land along the northeast edge of the island. The harbor is a small one, but a sanctuary none the less whose dimensions are about 700 yards long by 600 wide and 20 feet deep. As the days perceptibly shorten in the fall, ice begins to form around solid objects on these calm days. Intricate patterns of thin-layered crystals attach themselves to the wooden hulls of the ships. Miniature icebergs drift among them, the whalers shut down for the eight months of hard weather soon to arrive hammering the coast with winds up to 100 miles-per-hour with temperatures of seventy below. The permanent icepack is less than sixty miles to the north. Winter even in July is never far away. Snow squalls are already common, usually racing in from sea by late afternoon and sending everyone dashing for shelter from the sharp sting of the slicing particles of ice.

Some of the ships in the harbor are three-masted 85 to 110 feet long. They also are equipped with diesel engines of between 70 and 90 horsepower. The rest of the vessels are older two-masted schooners and hold smaller engines that are more for maneuvering and crossing tranquil waters, an uncommon situation in the far north. This limits their range on the harsh seas of the high Arctic where tacking across the wind, let alone trying to point even a few degrees into it, is more often than not, impossible in rough seas with waves over thirty feet and hell-bent full-gale-force blasts of wind.

The *Narwhal* is typical of the larger ships in the harbor. It was launched at New Bedford, Mass in 1842 when whaling was at its peak. In 37 voyages nearly 70 years she's traveled more leagues of the world's oceans than any other American whaling ship in history. The *Narwhal* is a full-rigged ship of 351 tons, measured 111 feet from stem to stern, and carries a complete suit of light sails in addition to her working canvas. To pursue the whales that are her quarry she carries six sturdy whaleboats. At the time of her launching she was considered state-of-the-art and could still hold her own with any whaling vessel found in Pauline Bay today.

On shore dozens of native canoes and kayaks litter the area as though an armada of downsized craft washed ashore on a high tide that was exacerbated by severe weather. The craft are beached haphazardly, lying at all angles – on their sides, bottoms up, tops up, bows pointing to sea, angling to inland or along the shore – next to casks of whale oil, engine fuel, bales of furs, and piles of off-loaded coal and scavenged timber to be used for heating the island buildings. Large, curved rib bones from bowhead whales and smaller ones from Belugas are piled high near a weathered tin storehouse called the "bone house." There is about one ton of bone per mature bowhead and at the going rate of five dollars per pound each whale is worth $10,000 for this material alone.

Hundreds of huskies and assorted mixed breeds of

curious and exotic lineage are chained to iron posts pounded deep into the hard ground wherever open permits. Inuits, whites, Kogmollick Eskimos – the men with labrets hanging from pierced lower lips and the women with tattooed chins, and several Loucheaux roam among the supplies and the rough buildings, most of which are crude structures made from chunks of sod, windowless with a chimney for cooking and heating fires inside the pungently aromatic, often filthy, dwellings. The Indians are shorter than the whites. Five-foot-seven is tall. Most of the aboriginal men are around five-three and the women less than five feet. The mix of different sizes lends a curious, carnival air to this human mélange that circles and surges along the shoreline. Native tents of animal hides, often decorated with designs of whales, seals, fish, the sun and planets, all drawn with pigments made from melted animal fats and tinted with soil, berries or even caribou blood, are pitched in among whalebones and decaying Arctic char that litter the shore. The air smells of salt, rendered whale blubber, fresh and rotting fish, and smoke from the smoldering fires of beached wood that is often still damp from its journey down the Mackenzie River and across the saltwater to Herschel. A constant din of howling dogs, yelling and chatting aboriginals and whites fills the air, creating an atmosphere of European Dark Ages mayhem now visited upon early twentieth century Beaufort Sea region.

Rare skins of wolverine or prime marten are bartered by trappers recently down from distant mountains ranges not delineated on any maps, unknown lands only rarely traveled by these solitary eccentrics. Natives hawk fish that are displayed in rows upon the bottoms of their upturned canoes. Tobacco, coffee, tea, barley flour, ammunition, rifles, calico, all of this and more is used as currency at this raucous, haphazard, open-air market. Soaring above and cavorting through the chaos are thousands of birds. Glaucous gulls, jaegers, black guillemots, Lapland longspurs and phalaropes are the most abundant among this mixture of so many species. The beating of wings and the wild, screeching cries mix with the human-generated din and the noise of the dogs – the sounds of life unrestrained, undisciplined, wildly unchecked. No one will ever accuse Pauline Cove of lacking energy or of not always persisting in a daylight state of constant motion. Evenings and deep night are only slightly slower paced, especially in the perpetual daylight of summer.

Farther back from shore on the slightest of rises of this nearly featureless island of less than eighty square miles, a barren ground that is devoid of all trees and most vegetation save for ancient lichens and mosses, stands the Northwest Mounted Police post. The place is a simple compound of headquarters, barracks, storage shack that serves double duty as a kennel, and the supply cache, all of the structures made of thick wooden planks fashioned from timber shipped down from the forests of the upper Mackenzie and from the occasional weathered gray trunks of giant spruce that have made the journey on their own during the spates of spring runoff. The gaps between timbers are chinked with a caulk of mud, clay and fine sand. Heavily-braced plank roofs are covered in pine bark and then a thick layer of sod cut from a bog located in the interior of Herschel, followed by dirt and then more sod. A design that is weather tight no matter the outside conditions.

The island is covered in a dense matting of tundra greens, the heather and grass sprinkled with colorful wildflowers for two months of the year. But by this time in autumn the ground cover has shifted to shades of rust, copper, darkest scarlet and burnt orange. Water seeps from the spongy ground and forms shallow ponds that spawn ice-cold, clear springs that rush down to the sea. Fifty to seventy-five miles distant on the mainland, the Romanzof Mountains rise dark blue beneath a sky of lighter blue covering a sea of aquamarine shading to gem-like beryl in the shallows. Small waves ripple the surface of the ever-present swell that washes in from the north in rolling liquid mounds that are barely perceptible within the enormity of the setting.

The whaling ships planning to spend the winter at Herschel carry an esoteric crew consisting of a combination of perhaps more than forty whalers from faraway locations that include Norway, England, Scotland, Denmark, France, the eastern U.S., even Iceland, and perhaps as many as fifteen natives to serve as hunters and seamstresses, fifty or more huskies to pull dog sleds, and the wife and children of the captain. Rank has its privileges, though a captain must pay a ship's owner $1,000 for this luxury of familial bliss. The winter of 1894-95 was the first season when families were allowed in the fleet. After leaving supplies at Herschel around mid-August, the whalers sail west for several weeks of hunting. As whaling tapers off the ships head for the sanctuary of Pauline Cove, normally by the beginning of October at the latest in preparation for the frozen lockup of the region's waters. The crews cover the ships' decks with an insulation of sod blocks, and build sod houses for the ship's inhabitants.

As the ice closes in, everyone faces what must soon feel like interminable and never-ending boredom and loneliness from October until the following May – a murders' row of cold, dark months. With five hundred men housed in close quarters, problems are inevitable. In past years drinking, desertion, and fighting were common, though since Inspector Macdonald's arrival to the port in 1908 the ensuing three years have experienced a steady decrease in these forms of debauchery until they are virtually non-existent. Rape, murder, public intoxication, all are dealt with immediately and harshly. A number of men, including an Inuit who sliced the throat of a whaler in a drunken brawl one winter night two years ago, have been tried, convicted and publicly hanged during the past three years.

When word reached Macdonald from Constable McIntire, who was on watch at the time of the slaying, concerning the murder by the Inuit, he immediately hitched a team of dogs to his sled. With a crack of his whip and the yell of "Hiyah," he started out after the fleeing Indian in the dead of night around two a.m. with only a few stars that appeared and disappeared behind the ragged cloud cover that presaged the approach of a snow storm. The Inspector had little trouble following the tracks made by the murderer's dogs and sled runners. Despite his half-hour head start, Macdonald steadily closed the distance between the two. He'd become a skilled sled and dog handler during his years of service with the NWMP both in the Alberta-British Columbia region and in the Arctic. He could keep up with anyone and break fresh trail through deep powder as well as any man.

His lead dog, sensing the nearness of the quarry, pushed even harder, spurring the other six dogs along with his enthusiasm. Macdonald closed to within thirty yards and yelled for the Inuit to halt. When this didn't work, he fired two shots from his Colt Service revolver ahead and just to the right of the man. The bullets kicked up snow and ice and caused the fleeing Indian to turn around and notice Macdonald's presence for the first time. The Inuit redoubled his efforts at escape, cracking a long whip over the heads and across the flanks of his shrieking dogs who were frantically churning their way across the wind-blown and crusted snow. The Indian kept going so the Inspector fired at the man while coursing along the uneven surface that conceals small pressure ridges caused by colliding ice sheets. Both men, running at a fair rate of speed, nearly upended several times when they bounced and lurched over these obstructions. Macdonald aimed for the fugitive's legs, striking both of them in the thigh and also hitting the man in the buttocks as three of the four shots he fired found their marks. The Inuit fell to the snow bleeding profusely and screaming in pain.

Macdonald was upon him in seconds. He secured the man's hands with a length of rope, bandaged his wounds as best he could, loaded him on his sled, and covered him with caribou hide blankets. He retrieved the other sled, re-aligned the dogs and started them back to Pauline Cove. He pushed his own team slightly ahead. The other group followed along in their wake. By four a.m. all were back at the settlement, the prisoner in the infirmary having his wounds attended to by a surgeon from one of the whaling ships. Macdonald saw to the dogs of both teams before checking on the injuries of the prisoner. He next walked over to headquarters in the below zero temperatures, the sky still dark in the brief days of winter. He filed formal written charges and wrote his report of the night's activities.

All this was only another day in the life of a Northwest Mountie far above the Arctic Circle. When the Inuit had recovered sufficiently from his wounds to stand trial, he was convicted and then hanged at noon the following day from a wooden gallows constructed near the waterfront by the bone house. Everyone turned out to watch the stern punishment which was intended as an object lesson for aboriginals and whites alike concerning Mountie authority and adherence to locals laws.

The stockade was frequently packed with those found guilty of public intoxication, theft and fighting, though these numbers of prisoners are decreasing as the Mounties instill law and order to the port.

More productive activities, though not commonly practiced, include the men playing baseball and soccer, skiing on the ice, and putting on plays and minstrel shows. The presence of women and children seems to reduce tensions. The wives organize card parties, dances, birthday, and holiday celebrations. The cabins are often decorated with lanterns and colored lights. At one gathering, a three-piece band played and ice cream, cake, beer, and cigars were served. Not Paris or New York but certainly not the violence-ridden, drunken, plague-infested, debauched port of years gone by.

Inspector Macdonald and Constable John Galpin stand on the front porch of Mountie headquarters taking in the view below them on the morning of the first day of October. The weather is clear, dead calm and crisp, conditions that belie the foul weather that can and will sweep down on Pauline Cove at any time now. A rime of frost covers the boats, structures and detritus that cover the beach. Indians, trappers and whalers are already moving around the waterfront setting up displays of freshly-caught fish, hauling coils of rope, rolling barrels of oil or fuel to and fro, talking in groups of two, three or more, feeding dogs and participating in other activities that seem to be as much busy work spawned by the ambient energy of the port as anything else.

"It is difficult to believe that all of this," and Macdonald waves an arm across the expanse of frenetic behavior before him, "now passes for order here these days. Three years ago drunkenness, fisticuffs, arguments, general acrimony were the rule of the day," said the Inspector. "We've done good work here corporal. Damned good work. And soon we'll take a temporary leave of all of this bucolic behavior," and Macdonald laughs aloud at this comment. He's nearly six feet tall with a thick mustache and full head of red hair that is going gray even at the early age of forty-one. When he laughs the sound rises from deep with in his broad chest and booms forth like a cannon shot. "We'll have the opportunity to travel the clean snows of the mountains and frozen rivers. Then we'll spend several weeks in Dawson City catching up on all that's happened these past years in the world that exists outside of our far northern realm. And, of course, there are the countless luxuries and delights of Dawson to be factored into our stay."

"Yes, Inspector, I agree," said Galpin. He's nearly the same height as Macdonald though about twenty pounds lighter. His auburn-colored hair is already showing signs of receding. "We've accomplished much here. I'm looking forward to the trip south and our time in the town. It will be a pleasure to visit Divisional Headquarters once again. To dine on their excellent table fair, to smoke good Cuban cigars and drink fine French brandy once again. And to try our skills on their new billiard table. Well, at least new since we've been down that way. And certainly an improvement over our table. The felt's gone bare and putting backspin on a shot is more a function of luck or God's will than anything. I hope to purchase new felt when we're down there."

Macdonald turned and looked directly into Galpin's eyes.

"Corporal, are you sure, are you confident, that you can see us through the canyons and passes that lead to the Blackstone? Going through that country heading south may look a good deal different to your eyes than it did heading up from Dawson those times in the late fall of the years. Getting lost or even making an unnecessary detour of only a few days may well prove disastrous at that time of year. "

"I know my way," said Galpin in a firm, confident voice. He relights his ever-present pipe, drawing deeply several times until the harsh, rough-cut tobacco is burning evenly. The two men have long since smoked their store of quality tobacco and consumed their good scotch. Cheap rum and even cheaper tobacco are all they have left now. The supply ship with choice quality goods never made the trip from Vancouver up and along the northern coast of Alaska and the Yukon to their isolated port. This will be a thin winter if the natives fail to provide their usual abundance of game. "I'll make sure we reach our goal and in good time, too. I'm not up for dying quite yet. Too many things to accomplish in the coming years, like seeing our new landing and dock through to its completion next summer. The facility will give order to all of those ships sitting out there."

Macdonald holds the man's gaze, then nods once in acknowledgment. His thoughts turn to a similar question he was asked when he was a sergeant stationed in Edmonton. A question asked by his superior who had assigned him the task of breaking and making trail through the uncharted wilderness between that post and Fort Selkirk on the distant Yukon River.

~ ~ ~

Late winter of 1897 finds sergeant Macdonald posted at Fort Edmonton on the outskirts of the bustling northern community of the same name. Located on the Alberta prairie about 150 miles north of Calgary, which itself is about 150 miles north of the Canada-Montana border, the burgeoning city is undergoing a tremendous population growth fueled by the discovery of enormous deposits of oil and natural gas in the vicinity. Huge cattle ranches and wheat growing operations are also starting up across the open plains. Another reason for the growth is the city's accessibility to the outside world by train and by a series of trails that more resembled rough roads. Thousands of men drawn to the Klondike gold fields and many more interested in trapping in the fur-rich forests and mountains of the Yukon are pouring into Edmonton. The winter has been a particularly harsh one of constant snowstorms that sweep down from the Arctic and out from the Rocky Mountains one hundred miles to the west. Streets are ice covered and drifts still choke alleys and many side streets. Temperatures remain below zero for weeks straight and the wind blasts across the flat expanse of the Alberta prairie.

Macdonald is called into Superintendent Hungerford's office on the third floor of Rowand House, a four level log structure that is one of the most impressive of its kind in the country. Hungerford's office is covered with maps and two portraits of his father and grandfather who had also served in the NWMP. Thick wool rugs from India cover the floors. The furniture is of the finest burled walnut and thick leather shipped across the Atlantic from England. Macdonald is directed to a large chair with matching footstool located next to its twin in front of a stone hearth. A crackling fire offers warmth, cheerful light and an atmosphere of comfort. From west-facing windows Macdonald watches as the sun drops behind the far horizon of timbered hills. Since this is after daytime duty hours he is offered both a cigar and a glass of cognac. The sergeant accepts both gratefully. It is common knowledge that Hungerford smokes only the finest Cuban cigars and drinks only the finest of French brandy.

"I think that you'll find the Partagas to your liking," said the Inspector. He clips both of their cigars with a silver cutter then lights his carefully using three matches in a practiced ritual. Macdonald follows perceived protocol and nuance and does the same. Both men sip the cognac and puff on their cigars enjoying the richly exotic tastes of each. Life is good, even way out in the wilds of western Canada.

"I prefer the Piramide. Burns more evenly and cooler. Of course the cognac could be better, but one must make do out here," said the Inspector as he eyes the younger man through a haze of bluish smoke. A knot bursts on one of the logs sending a series of sparks up the chimney. "I'll come to the point. I'm giving you a most difficult assignment, but one I know you can handle with dispatch. I want you to assemble a group of six men counting yourself, as many horses as needed along with appropriate tools, supplies and rations to begin constructing a trail from Edmonton across what is largely unmapped subArctic wilderness stretching for more than 1,200 miles to Fort Selkirk in the Yukon. And I want you to take bearings along the way to update and add detail to the dreadful maps we have of that country. Most of the space is simply labeled 'Uncharted.' Dreadful. Damned dreadful in this day and age.

"You must go at the beginning of the warmer months to hack through bush that is in full leaf," said Hungerford. "This is the time of the year when most of the gold seekers will be trying to get to the gold fields. Admittedly tracking in the dead of winter would be easier, but those are the specifics of your assignment."

The order takes Macdonald by surprise. What Hungerford is asking will not just be difficult, it may well be impossible for six men to accomplish. Building a trail across the muskeg, near-impenetrable forests, rugged mountain ranges, huge lakes and wild rivers of Alberta, British Columbia and the Yukon District would seem inconceivable to most men. Still orders are orders and the sergeant never backs off a challenge, instead he meets them head on bringing his strong will to bear on the task.

As if reading his mind Hungerford says "I know that most people would consider this assignment folly, impossible, the orders of an intractable bureaucrat. To some extent I agree, but we're posted out here because we're the ones looked to by the politicians back east to get things done, to accomplish serious work. I believe, hell, I know that you're the man for this project. I have the ultimate faith in your ability and tenacity to see this one through to completion."

"Thank you, sir," said Macdonald. "I won't let you or the

Service down."

The sergeant realizes that thousands of stampeders, most of them with little or no wilderness survival skills, have already struck out and are leaving in a steady stream on a daily basis, trail or no trail. Many of them become lost, discouraged, stranded or dead within a few hundred miles of the city. The Canadian government wants an end put to this disorder and disaster. Macdonald is being given the assignment to accomplish this goal. He will get to travel through virgin country and, if successful, advance his career within the service immeasurably. Macdonald understands that the original order has come from the prime minister's office in Ottawa via dispatch to the superintendent. He also knows that the current power structure is both imperious and impatient. That its leaders brook no delays or excuses, let alone failure of even the smallest proportions. He realizes that Hungerford chose him because he is considered by his commander to be the most reliable and motivated member of the Mounties in not only Fort Edmonton, but provincial Alberta as well. This is a high honor. Macdonald also appreciates the fact that the superintendent has a great deal riding on the outcome of this mission. Not carrying out these orders successfully could well harm both of their careers in the NWMP.

"You are also given the power to arbitrarily settle any disputes that you encounter among the stampeders along the way to the Yukon River and Fort Selkirk," said Hungerford as he pours more of what the sergeant considers to be an exceptional cognac into both of their brandy snifters. "I'll not mince words here. If you prove successful, I'll be transferred back to Ottawa. A posting I desire greatly. Literally above all else. And you'll be promoted to the rank of Inspector. Something for both of us in this, eh, Macdonald?"

The sergeant agrees.

The two men spend another hour working out various details involving these orders. When Macdonald leaves the Superintendent's office he is feeling a bit drunk from the cognac, the good cigar and the heady awareness that his dream of reaching the Yukon is about to be realized.

Macdonald decides to select only men that are relatively new to the Mounties. Men with no more than four years experience but no less than two. Sufficient time to learn some of the rules, tricks and the code of discipline that make the NWMP respected throughout the Canadian Northwest, but not so long that they will be set in their ways. Hopefully they will still be malleable for the tough track that awaits them and the spontaneous thinking and problem solving that will be needed to see this assignment through to a positive conclusion. Macdonald's first choice is John Galpin, a promising Constable with only two years of service. Macdonald noticed the man right off as soon as he arrived in Edmonton. Galpin is a self-starter who can follow, and more importantly, apply orders to fluctuating conditions. He is trustworthy and a hard worker. Both traits the sergeant has observed over the course of tasks that included improvements on the rough road that accessed the post, settling disputes among the often drunk and violent citizenry and maintaining order in a community that may be the size of a city but is still little more than a wild west frontier town filled with trappers, grifters, gamblers, thieves, professional women, and drifters. Macdonald believes that he will need a man of Galpin's character and abilities to help him keep order and moral among his crew while in the midst of what he imagines are going to be severe, if not brutal, conditions along the way, that he will require a right-hand man to back him up when the going turns tough as it surely will.

"I'm prepared for this assignment whenever you're ready to head out, sir," said Galpin one evening a couple of weeks before the planned start of the assignment in mid-April. "I'm honored and excited to be selected. Whatever you need, I can round up for you. I've access to either the supplies we need or to men who can requisition those goods for us."

The enthusiastic constable also makes out a list containing nine names of potential recruits for the trail-making duty. Macdonald and Galpin devote the next several nights outlining a proposed course on the crude maps that are available for the country they are to cross. They also make an extensive list of provisions, and conduct interviews among the nine men on Galpin's list. Picking four proves difficult. They are all good, self-motivated individuals who want a taste of real adventure. This assignment promises that and more.

Eventually all is in readiness. Two hours before dawn on April 30th the contingent of six Mounties along with a Metis Indian named Baptiste Trudeau, who is hired to handle the pack string of 43 horses plus the seven ridden by the men, leaves the Edmonton post and heads west beneath the stars. The air is cold, below zero. A fresh breeze is running down from the north, hinting at a Chinook. By midmorning the temperature has climbed into the mid-fifties. The north wind racing along the eastern edge of the Canadian Rockies is now a full-blown Chinook, a western weather phenomenon that causes rapid warming, often sixty or more degrees in a couple of hours, that melts deep drifts of snow and dries the ground with its fast-moving energy. Chinooks have been known to boost temperatures from 20 below zero in the middle of February to the upper forties in a little more than an hour. While their winds are intense, they are always welcomed by residents along the Rocky Mountain Front. Any relief from the months of heavy snow and bone-chilling cold is considered a godsend, a respite from often killing weather.

Initially the contingent makes good time, over twenty miles each of the first two days, as they travel through open country where streams are lined with cottonwoods. The country gradually shifts to a forest of pine, poplar and birch with willow and alder choking stream banks. In the early going the way is marked by wagon wheel indentations, horse hooves and the steps of eager men as the path resembles a two-track road leading to one of the ranches near Edmonton. Gradually this diminishes to a well-trodden course, then merely a worn trail through the gathering wilderness. They encounter would-be gold seekers stranded alongside the way, gear and bodies already broken down. They pass a steady flow of men returning to Edmonton, the faint-hearted dregs of the human flood destined for the Klondike. The Mounties hack large blazes shoulder-height on the trunks of prominent trees to mark the way for future travelers, some of whom pass the men in the early going, clearly in a hurry to reach the imagined Eldorado of the Yukon gold fields. The stream of adventurers, most of them inexperienced city dwellers doomed to death or worse as Macdonald views the situation, runs nearly all year long. The tide only halts, and this briefly, in times of brutally cold storms, but resumes its relentless flow as soon as the bad weather moves on to the east. Individuals eager to reach the ore diggings and the imagined easy pickings of gold-nugget wealth that is rumored to abound in the streams and rivers surrounding Dawson City seem to exist in a never-ending supply.

When the group comes to marshy areas it cuts down spruce, fir or other pine species, preferring these to birch or willow because the resin in the conifers retards rot and insect damage. These they saw into lengths of logs wide enough to accommodate supply wagons that travel the first stages of the route. The timbers are laid cross-wise along the moist areas to facilitate travel. If large rocks are lying around nearby they are piled on to the edges of the logs to help hold them in place. Large trees that stand directly in the most advantageous path are felled. As the Mounties and Baptiste move west by Northwest the land becomes more contoured as hills covered with increasingly thick forest now slow their progress. The Metis is skilled with driving horses, but even a small remuda such as this one presents difficulties and tries the patience of the wrangler as the large animals have trouble moving among the tightly-packed stands of "dog fur" lodgepole pine and climbing over the multitude of deadfalls. Often a dozen animals will clear an obstruction easily, but then one recalcitrant beast will balk at moving forward, a downed tree taking on terrifying dimensions in its mind. Whinnying and rearing on hind legs, the animal proceeds to spook the following horses who buck, rear and raise a ruckus that seems to presage the end of the world. Baptiste spends as much as an hour coaxing the horses over the fearsome obstacle then pushes on as hard as possible to close the distance between himself and the Mounties who never let up in their relentless trail-making work. Before they set out, Baptiste told Macdonald to leave all but the most dire troubles related to the horses in his hands. If he needs help, he'll yell, otherwise the six Mounties are to proceed at their own pace. He explains that there is no need to complicate commonplace trail dilemmas that the horses' easily riled brains are entirely capable of twisting into full-scale disasters without the help of the Mounties' assistance. He adds that "This is something horses are quite good at," laughs and heads for the fort's corral.

At rivers like the Pembina and Paddle, small by this country's dimensions, but still pushing enough current to be dangerous, the men clear wide landings along the banks, construct sturdy rafts and stout bull boats – circular craft made with a birch framework covered in moose hides with the seams waterproofed with pine resin. Moose are plentiful along the way, as are deer, and black bear that are a constant nuisance as the scavenging creatures continually try and raid the men's stores of bacon, pemmican and sugar. The party has little trouble shooting the moose or other animals for the skins and to satisfy enormous appetites of men who burn 10,000 calories or more as they hack their way through the virgin countryside. They leave one raft and bull boat on each side of each river they cross.

By the time they reach the tiny settlement of Whitecourt at the headwaters of the Athabasca River that forms just below the confluence of the Athabasca and McCleod rivers the men have already covered more than eighty miles in ten hard-working days. An excellent pace that Macdonald knows will not continue as they near the steep flanks of the Rocky Mountains. This stretch was something of a shakedown cruise that offered Macdonald a chance to see the strengths and weaknesses of his crew. The ten days also rounded the men into better shape than they were when they left Edmonton, which was lean and tough to begin with.

While the Athabasca is already wide and deep at this location, the current, though strong, is not whitewater or whirlpool treacherous. The men build sturdy flatboats, one for each side of the river. These are nearly twenty-five feet long and ten feet wide with gunwales of almost two feet to help keep men and gear dry during the crossings. Clearings on both shores have already been chopped out of the bush and are maintained by the outpost's inhabitants. Macdonald and his men spend a couple of Sunday's – a term for non-traveling days of rest – at Whitecourt. The time is used reorganizing gear based on the past days' experiences, repairing any damaged equipment and assessing how the expedition has done so far. To Macdonald's and Galpin's way of thinking, quite well.

For the next three weeks the men push their way through dense forest, long stretches of muskeg and across normally small creeks now rising towards full flood as an uncommonly mild spring triggers an early and severe snow melt. The warm temperatures, often in the mid-seventies, also release mosquito larvae from their icebound prisons, the bugs swarming in clouds of ravenous insects that cause both men and horses extreme misery. Working in swampy terrain while being enveloped with buzzing, biting mosquitoes is maddening labor. At times hellish. By the end of the day everyone is exhausted and in foul spirits. A ration of whiskey is as necessary as it is an enjoyable accompaniment to the men's evening's pipes smoked around a roaring bonfire that raises spirits and deters the mosquitoes.

They continue to cut down trees and brush, blaze trail, lay corduroy patches of logs and improve a ford across the Little Smoky River by removing a thick snag of washed down tree trunks and branches. A stick of dynamite loosens the tangle from a jumble of midstream boulders, the entire mess speeding down river in a scattered string of weathered and now blasted debris. When they must line supplies and horses across rushing creeks, they carve out the bush down to bare-earth openings that lead into and out of the cold water that within six weeks will have dropped to a trickle in many instances. But for now the tedious process of using strung ropes to cross the rushing waters is necessary. Game is everywhere. The number of moose, naturally mean-spirited and aggressive creatures, is often a problem, the men killing the animals as much to be able to continue with their task as for the rich meat. The bulls often charge the men, crashing through the forest and across the muskeg with murder on their minds. Macdonald is forced to assign one armed man the duty of guarding the others. Meat for camp is never a problem. A few gunshots, some butchering, and either stewing the meat in a kettle or grilling thick slabs of flesh over piles of hot coals is all that's needed these days. Every night is a feast for the ravenous crew.

They manage to build large rafts that ferry them across the wide Smoky River just below where it merges with the Simonette. Next they work up the steep hills surrounding the river through impressive stands of towering birch and then down rounded hills and back onto prairie and forest flatlands towards a wide notch that cuts between the Birch and Saddle hills. With luck they'll reach Fort St. John on the Peace River by the first week of June.

One morning while working their way across the Ksituan River, a unique sight, a ghostly white specter, greets the men. An albino moose, an enormous specimen of well over 2,000 pounds with a rack of more than seven feet, is grazing in an adjacent marsh area on aquatic plants. Baptiste pulls his rifle from its leather scabbard and fires four times. He hits the moose with each shot, as do Galpin and one of the constables. Perhaps nine bullets hammer the beast, that roars in a spray of water and masticated plant matter before crashing and thundering through the muskeg and uphill through the forest that begin a quarter-mile away. Baptiste and Galpin give chase, quickly dropping from their mounts at the tree line. They follow a thick blood trail for two miles, but this dries up and ends on top of a bare rock ridge. A sheer drop of more than a thousand feet on three sides confronts the two. The only way out is back the way they came. Galpin glasses the terrain below the precipice. He finds not a trace of the great white moose.

"Where did the moose vanish to?" asks Galpin. "It's not down there below, dashed on the stone. I couldn't miss its body on that bare rock. No way could it have survived a fall from here and wandered away into those trees down there. It didn't pass us by on our way up. It's just gone. Like it never existed to begin with."

Baptiste laughs and laughs. Then in the clearest of voices with no trace of his French accent he recites in a loud voice from Melville's *Moby Dick*:

"By heaven, man, we are turned round and round in this world, like yonder windlass, and Fate is the handspike ...Where do murderers go, man! Who's to doom, when the judge himself is dragged to the bar? But it is a mild, mild wind, and a mild looking sky; and the airs smells now, as if it blew from a far-away meadow; they have been making hay somewhere under the slopes of the Andes, Starbuck, and the mowers are sleeping among the new-mown hay. Sleeping? Aye, toil we how we may, we all sleep at last on the field. Sleep? Aye, and rust amid greenness; as last year's scythes flung down, and left in the half-cut swarths- Starbuck!"

Galpin stares at Baptiste, dumbstruck, mouth open, his eyes filled with astonishment.

Baptiste laughs again.

"I was trapped in a cabin years ago during a long, long winter along Hudson's Bay," said Baptiste. "There was little to do but run trap lines and try to keep warm. No whiskey and no women to fill a man's time. There was only one book on the shelf. The *Moby Dick* by Melville. I read it through several times and memorized those parts that mean something to me. The words seemed to be right for our little adventure, don't you think? I've heard tales of white moose, like Ahab's great white whale, but I never believed in either until now. Perhaps this is a sign of our impending success or maybe our failure. You think?"

Galpin shakes his head and the two return to the rest of the men to report the curious adventure, Galpin exclaiming that they have a learned man, a thespian, in their midst.

Macdonald catches the mischievous sparkle in the Frenchman's eyes and laughs aloud himself.

"It appears that we'll not want for amusement on this

little trek of ours, eh, Baptiste," said the sergeant.

"I think you may be right, sergeant," said Baptiste.

The men continue on their way with many miles of trail to hack, build and mark before they reach Fort St. John, a settlement of long history and importance to northwest Canada.

The arrival of fur traders brought change. From untouched wilderness a fort was raised. And over the past century a number separate trading posts have been built near the present location of Fort St. John, their comings and goings mimicking a solid land tide of human settlement, a pattern that repeats itself at locations through the north country. The first of these is Rocky Mountain House, constructed in 1791. It is the first white settlement on the mainland of British Columbia. It was located southwest of present Fort St. John, on the Peace River just upstream from the Moberly River. It closed in 1805. Fort d'Epinette was built in 1806 by the North West Company. Renamed Fort St. John in 1821 when the North West Company was bought by the Hudson's Bay Company. It was situated about 500 yards downstream from the mouth of the Beatton River, which at that time was called the Pine (*d'epinette* in French). It shut down in 1823. The Revillon Frères Company built a two-story cabin for trading in about 1806, but did it not remain long. Fort St. John, built in the 1860s, was located on the south side of the Peace River, directly south of the present community. It ceased operation in 1872. A new Fort St. John is built in 1872 and located on the north side of the river, across from the previous fort and is on the new trail to Fort Nelson. Many of the trading posts along the route receive their supplies from this outpost that is growing with each passing year and each surge of adventurers through the land.

As is common in the Northwest, the church was into the Peace River district quite early as well. In 1866, Bishop

Faraud, of the Oblates of Mary Immaculate, arrived to teach the Beaver Indians about God. Five years later, the Right Reverend William Carpenter Bompas held Anglican services in Fort St. John and Hudson Hope. By 1890, a small chapel had been built for worshippers at Fort St. John. And now the gold rush to the Klondike is affecting the region, as the Beaver Indians try and refuse access to the stampeders wishing to pass through their territory. While searching through the files contained in the Fort Edmonton library this past winter, Macdonald came across the following excerpt from a recent Annual Report of the North-West Mounted Police (NWMP) that describes the situation:

"Mr. Fox (the post manager) informs me that the Indians here at first refused to allow the white men to come through their country without paying toll...They threatened to burn the feed and kill the horses; in fact several times fires were started, but the head men were persuaded by Mr. Fox to send out and stop them. There is not doubt that the influx of whites will materially increase the difficulties of hunting by the Indians, and these people, who, even before the rush, were often starving from their inability and, more importantly, unwillingness to procure game on their own for themselves, will in future be in much worse condition. They are very likely to take what they consider a just revenge on the white men who have come, contrary to their wishes, and scattered themselves over their country. When told that if they started fighting as they threatened, it could only end in their extermination, the reply was, we may as well die by the white men's bullets as of starvation."

Macdonald's party reaches the Peace River opposite Fort St. John's midday in early June. The river is swollen from runoff pouring down from the Rocky Mountains now less than fifty miles away. They tower above the forested valley that drifts off to the foot of the uncharted peaks. Still more water melts and cascades from the Cassiar and Omineca Mountains hidden behind the Rocky Mountain massif. The Peace carries all of this through a canyon gap in the Rockies, the river's level thirty feet above its normal August flow. The roar of the rushing water dominates everything. The men must shout to be heard. The millions of cubic feet of water that pass by each minute vibrate through the rock along shore, up through the men's feet. The power of the Peace is awe-inspiring.

From the northern shore directly below the post two large boats start out towards the men. Lookouts in one of the fort's towers spot the crew as soon as they began dropping down the several-hundred foot bluffs that guard the river. A wide trail cuts back and forth through the forest of white birch now cloaked in the bright green leaves of spring. A warm breeze makes a steady rustling sound as it glides upriver.

The craft are nearly forty-feet long and fifteen wide, powered by engines that can't be heard above the din of the Peace. Columns of black smoke rise from each stack before being dispersed by the day's breeze. The boats have an open deck space for the first fifteen feet of their lengths, then cabins with small pilothouses on top. They angle upstream but the current sweeps them down below Macdonald into a large eddy that swings both boats neatly to shore directly in front of the men. One is called the *Shining Mountain* and the other the *Alberta*. Both craft fly the Canadian flag, the red background, the blue, red and whites of the Union Jack in the upper left-hand corner with the brightly colored crest flutter and shimmer in the wind. Baptiste guides the horses onto both boats with sharp yells and a cracking whip. The animals are terrified of the river, but fear the Frenchman's wrath and the sound of his whip snapping well above their flanks more. Macdonald sends two men along in the boats to help Baptiste.

The craft return in about an hour. The river has risen a couple of inches in this brief span, the chocolate water crashing by carrying trees and snags of over a hundred feet, and dead carcasses of sheep, moose, caribou. It as though the Peace is conducting a spring cleaning of its thousands of square miles of drainage. Just down river where the channel narrows to a quarter mile, standing waves created by the rock walls forcing the water through a confined space of limited capacity rise a dozen feet and more, the water arching its back like a gigantic bucking bronco before slamming down into the depression directly below with crashings like thunderclaps. Should one of the boats loose an engine and be swept over and into this mayhem, complete destruction and death would be the only outcome.

Macdonald and his men load their gear including several hundred pounds of moose meat they have remaining from a pair of kills the evening before. Crossing the river is a new, wild, exhilarating experience for the sergeant. The water pounds against the tall gunwales. He looks far upstream between the gap in the Rockies and catches a brief glimpse of the snow capped Ominecas. In a matter of a few days his men will be working along the shoreline of this river establishing marked portages and turning northward up the Finlay River in search of a pass over the unknown mountains of the Pacific-Arctic Divide and then down the Kechika River for possibly three-hundred miles to the mighty Liard River. From that point, whenever they reach it, the journey will turn truly tough, uncommonly difficult. The boats' crews are skilled, efficient. They effect the crossing with little fan fare, no wasted effort and without incident.

Fort St. John is bustling with activity. It is the largest settlement for two hundred miles in any direction. The stockade walls of the post contain Mountie headquarters, a jail, barracks, mess hall, black smith, infirmary and extensive stables. The expedition's horses are taken here and attended to by the constables under Baptiste's gruff but also joking guidance. The animals have their packs removed, coats curried and are fed a healthy ration of oats from the storage bin that is near-full from a recent supply boat that originated at the settlement of Peace River far downstream. Also within the walls that have been expanded twice in the past 18 months are a number of Hudson Bay Company buildings including a trading post-company store. There are also several smaller private businesses including a hide tanner and a small hotel and restaurant known as The Regent. Outside adjacent to the twelve-foot log walls is Faille's Saloon a town, open at all hours, but the fort's gates are closed and barricaded at 10 p.m., a consideration many boarder's at The Regent have failed to factor into their liquid evenings leading to a night sleeping on the rough wood-plank floor of the tavern. Albert Faille is a former trapper, one of the first men to travel through Peace River country. With the more or less permanent establishment of Fort St. John, Faille turned to an easier and more profitable way of earning money, liquor. He opened his establishment several years ago after selling several pounds of dust and gold nuggets and a load of furs the quality of which is still talked about in Alberta. He used part of the money to build the saloon, more to stock it with whiskey, rum and ale. He deposited the remaining money in the Bank of Canada in Edmonton. Business has been good to the sixty-year-old man who is now wealthy, even by big city terms.

After reporting to the camp commander, Inspector Hayes, Macdonald sees that his men are settled in their temporary quarters and then does the same himself in a private room next to Hayes' quarters. The four walls seem confining after the weeks on the trail through the wilderness where the only individuals they saw outside of Whitecourt were a band group of Metis working the Pembina in a pair of canoe-like pirogue dugouts made from large birch trunks. The craft were weighed down with moose hind quarters. Macdonald plans to spend three days resting, fixing gear, seeing that the horses are in good shape and learning all he can about the country lying west and north of him. He's heard that Faille is the one to talk to. In the morning following breakfast that's where Macdonald plans to visit. Despite the enclosed space, his room is comfortable with a fine bed set in eastern linens and blankets, a woven rug from England and a writing table and chair. The window is made of even glass with only modest distortion. All of this is luxury for this far from any major city.

After a leisurely dinner that features oysters, burgundy, lamb chops and asparagus from the post's garden, followed by the usual cigars and brandy with Hayes, pleasant hours spent filling in the Inspector on the progress with trail making so far and also gleaning any travel information that he can, Macdonald retires to his room, sleeps soundly until 5 a.m., awakes, bathes, dresses, eats breakfast, checks on his men, talks with Baptiste about the state of the horses – they are doing well, and then spends two hours updating his journal. By mid-morning he is off to see Faille. He passes through the open gate and covers the brief distance down a boardwalk to the saloon. The log structure is already open and several trappers are seated at a table near one of the front windows. Macdonald can see through the open door that five men are playing cards, drinking beers and pouring whiskey from a ceramic pitcher into tin cups. The figures appear dark, shadowy, indistinct in the haze of pipe and cigar smoke. There is loud banter and laughter involving the game and various shortcomings related to each of them. The sounds bounce through the door's opening. A pair of windows, each divided into a dozen framed rectangles of glass, are set in the log wall on either side of the entrance. An engraved sign hangs from the roof that covers a wooden deck. It says "Faille's Tavern." Benches are built into the wall just the proper distance for a man to put his feet up on the railings made of birch limbs. What really catches Macdonald's eye are the two flower boxes below the windows. They are painted dark green as are the slatted storm shutters. Marigolds and peonies grow in colorful profusion – orange, yellow, red, cerulean, pink, white, robin's egg blue.

A wiry man with a thick red beard is wiping down the mahogany bar with a clean white rag. The premises are remarkably clean, even by NWMP standards. The sergeant is impressed. Brass kerosene lanterns hang from cross beams beneath the arched ceiling and two are glowing on the counter behind the bar.

"What will it be, Inspector?" asks Faille as he pours the man a mug of black coffee. They formally introduce each other over a firm shaking of hands. "I've tea, but this is in all the way from Jamaica. An excellent blend. Unusual fare for these parts, you must agree. I heard that you and your men arrived yesterday and I suspected that you'd drop by before you pushed on."

Macdonald takes a sip. Aromatic, spicy, rich. He's not had coffee of this quality since his last trip to Ottawa. Faille is rising rapidly in the eyes of the Mountie. Behind the bar a mirror runs the length of the wall, the clean glass surrounded by an ornate, hand-carved frame of griffins, dolphins, and eagles with fierce talons. Macdonald notices that his faced is tanned and already weathered as he checks his reflection. Several bottles of scotch are next to a register of flat black metal with silver keys.

"Excuse me a moment," said Faille and he moves over to a stone hearth and places a couple of three-foot logs on the fire. The day promises warmth and sunshine, but is still cool enough for frost to cling to the grass.

"You've spent some money and invested a fair amount of your time outfitting this place. I like the flowers. A pleasant touch to be sure," said Macdonald. "The mahogany and the mirror are something one wouldn't expect to find even in Edmonton or Calgary. And the scotch...well, I'll have a dram of the Pulteney if you will."

"Good man. 'The Manzanilla of the North,' they say of its salty tang," said Faille as he uncorks the bottle. He pours a healthy shot for the two of them and leaves the bottle on the bar. "Thank you for your compliments. Here's to a fine day and many more of the same. I wish this for you and your men, and an even finer trip through this country."

The two men drink and Faille pours more of the bright amber liquid in each crystal glass that seems to sparkle as if lit from within.

"That's why I'm here. I've been given to understand from a source in Edmonton and another at Whitecourt that no man knows the country behind the Rockies as well as you. I'm headed up the Finlay and then the Techieca establishing a trail for our gold-lusting brethren. And then down the Kechika for the Liard. Any information on that way will be appreciated. My men and I have a long distance to cover before we reach Fort Selkirk on the Yukon by the end September, God willing."

"God willing is right," said Faille. "There's some severe terrain you'll be cutting your way through and climbing over, though working your way up the trench between the mountains is a far easier passage then continuing north along the eastern edge of these mountains and then trying to cross over west of Fort Nelson. That passage can be accomplished, but it is many more miles and would cost you an extra two weeks.

"I must say that I believe that the best service you can

do for these inexperienced men passing through here chasing a fool's gold is to barricade the road out of Edmonton. Arrest all who pass its barrier because at best they are bound for poverty," said Faille. "Baring that, mark well and establish clearly portages up the Finlay and the Techieca. There are canyons filled with reefs and cascades that no man can conquer even in low water and never in a wild man's dream during flood conditions. Even lining canoes along the edges of these torrents is dangerous, often deadly work. As for the portages, they often climb steeply up rock banks that are most surely related to cliffs of our homeland highlands."

"Aye, that's what I was imagining," said Macdonald. "Have you some specifics I can write down for the journey?"

"If you were a small party moving through the country and not establishing a trail I would recommend that you obtain a pair of sixteen-foot canoes," said Faille. "They handle the current well, are relatively easy to line or portage around cascades and they carry a fair amount of gear. Only in a few places would you need to frog the canoes, to get out and push and pull them with the strength of your legs and arms. But since you're moving overland with horses, here's what I can offer you in the way of information.

"You'll need to climb the cliff below the rapids that head at the Wicked River a days march along the shore from the gap in the mountains on our Peace. From the joining of the Parsnip coming in from the south with the Finlay you'll have a hard pull through the trees and thick undergrowth to Fort Grahame, though there are no real hazards. You may replenish some goods at the Hudson Bay store there, but keep a sharp eye on the Sikani that hang around the post. The lazy bastards would rather steal from whites than hunt and fish for their own food.. They are easily intimidated face to face, but come night or when you are away from your goods, they move as fast as weasels.

"From there the Finlay is wide and sluggish. Maybe two miles in spots. Stay to the eastern shore. Such as it is, there's a trail and if you were to come by boat you'd to cheat the prevailing wind. It's an old and not often used Indian trail that is still barely visible. It is covered in deadfall and needs work."

The sergeant takes all of this down. While Faille speaks, he also works on a map of the country the men are discussing, marking in mountain ranges, rivers and other landmarks on a thick sheet of rag paper as the barman adds details to his narrative. The men finish their drinks. Faille refills both the glasses and Macdonald's mug with fresh coffee.

"To cover the next stretch will require at least a week to reach the Kwadacha River that heads beneath the great glacier that covers the western slopes of Mt. Smythe. And you'll have to push hard most of each day to cover the distance in those seven days. About a half-mile up the river it shallows and you can ford your horses, even in runoff. From there work up the Finlay until you reach the Techieca. Stay along the eastern side of this one, too. There was a wildfire in that country two summer's ago. The land is now mostly a wasteland packed ash and soot and of blackened deadfalls. New scrub pines are coming back and they make traversing the place difficult, but you'll manage. The other shore is impassable due to sheer rock walls and cliffs.

"The horses should be able to negotiate the place and the mountains as well, especially with this Baptiste with you," said Faille while hand-grinding more of the oily, black coffee beans, the rich smell filling the saloon. "His reputation with horses reaches even this far from the prairie. The valley climbs steeply to the river's head, but your men can make trail through the timber. Hard labor, but it can be accomplished. From there a sheep, goat and Indian trail traverses the rocky slopes that give way to the

Kechika.

"More of the same to the Liard. Stay on the high timbered southern shore of that fearsome river. Indian trails partially mark the way, but you'll be on your own until you reach the Liard headwaters divide that drops down into Pelly River country. You can build rafts and float down to Fort Selkirk, though there are some stretches of cascade and broken water to contend with. Improving the trail on the southern shore would aid the stampeders considerably. Game is plentiful as are fish in all of the rivers. The grayling, Dolly Vardon and trout."

In this way Macdonald passes the rest of the day with Faille gaining invaluable information that it took the saloon owner decades to acquire through every season filled with of all sorts of weather in uncharted country. Faille serves a steady stream of trappers passing through or staying near the Fort during this conversation with Macdonald. No Indians are allowed in to purchase any liquor or even to hang around the premises killing time, though several can be seen loitering outside in front of the entrance. No alcohol to the aboriginals is the most severely enforced law at St. John and the rest of the territory.

"Thank you Faille," said Macdonald and he begins to place some money on the counter.

"Not here. Not this day Sergeant," said Faille, pushing the coins back to the Mountie and handing him the rolled up map. "It's been my pleasure and I hoped my words will prove of some small value to you on your mission. God's speed to you and your men. I wish I could accompany you. I miss that country. I'll be here waiting for your return."

The two men shake hands and Macdonald retraces the steps to his quarters inside the confining walls of the fort. The sergeant looks to the Rocky Mountains and the sun now setting behind them.

"I've come a long way since Scotland all those years

ago," he thinks, and he recalls the death of his parents in a fire that destroyed that pleasant past when he was sixteen. Macdonald had been out roaming the highlands for several days hunting, fishing, exploring and camping on his own. He did this whenever time allowed. He loved walking through the grasses, mosses and heather of the uplands and fishing the creeks that poured down from the rocky summits, little waters filled with native brown trout, colorful fish of deep brown honeyed flanks and crimson spots. When he returned from his outing, all was gone. The past that made up so much of his life, all of the loving memories were incinerated. A chimney fire exploded through the two-century old home the night before burning his family in their sleep. The image of the remaining charred timbers that once were the sturdy frame of the structure, of the two blackened chimneys standing like battered sentinels waiting for his return, that vision is all that remains for him now. The lurid memory haunts his dreams. He had no other family in the country. They'd all died or had traveled across the Atlantic to begin new lives in Canada. Stricken and truly alone for the first time in his life, Macdonald made a quick decision, a characteristic that would serve him well in the coming years. He gathered a few belongings and a bag of gold coins he'd been adding to one at a time as his labors around the village were paid for, money he'd been saving to go off to the university in Edinburgh, and trekked down from the highlands to the coast and the port city of Inverness. It didn't take him long to locate and sign on to crew for a steamer bound for another St. John's, this one the bustling capital city of the Canadian province located on a deep bay of the Atlantic. He worked as a mess boy and assistant to the cook along with doing any other menial task such as cleaning decks, coiling rope and shining the bright work. He didn't care. Nothing mattered to him except putting distance between him and

Scotland. These labors paid for his passage and earned a few extra dollars as well. When he reached St. John's he located a boarding house and found work on the nearby docks. When he turned seventeen he enlisted in the Mounted Police. Except for one incidence of intoxication during his first year, his record has been spotless, exemplary.

Since the loss of those most dear to him, Macdonald has been unwilling or unable to get truly close to anyone. Whenever the beginnings of a friendship or a relationship with a woman arise, Macdonald closes down and walks away both emotionally and physically. The thought of growing close or even dependent on another person, on someone who could vanish from his life in an unexplained, unfair instant, terrifies him. He vowed years ago to never put himself in a position that held the possibility for so much pain. He prefers his solitary internal existence, never wanting to again feel the agony he'd experienced that dreadful morning in Scotland more than a decade ago. The only woman he ever loved, Emily, a gorgeous, kind person from a wealthy Montreal family, he left with nothing more than a note saying that he'd been assigned to Edmonton and would see her when he next returned on leave. He'd added that for now he felt that it was best if they put their engagement on hold. That this would be best for both of them. The decision came to him in a flash of awakening from a nightmare of reliving the death of his family. The choice was clear. Easy to make. Spontaneous. That was ten years ago. He'd not written Emily since his leaving despite many notes from her pleading with him to come back, to at least explain his actions. Actions he could not fully understand, let alone define for himself. All he knew from the depths of his soul is that he never wanted to experience the hell of the loss that he'd gone through in Scotland. Eventually the letters from her dwindled to a perfunctory note once or twice a year, then stopped altogether. Macdonald scarcely noticed. The Mounties and the Canadian Northwest are his life now, the two dominate and direct his actions, plans and dreams.

"All of life is connected, if only we take the time to look," he thinks as he enters his room.

Macdonald and his men follow the map that Faille drew that day in the saloon and they adhere to his verbal direction as they work up the Peace to its junction with the Finlay. Then they cut and hack through the bush, and set corduroy bridgings in moist seeps encountered on the more than one hundred mile slog up the river's drainage. Game is plentiful. The crew eats well. They replenish some goods including salt, an unexpected find of a tin of black pepper and even more exotic find of a case of canned peaches at Fort Grahame. All the time they keep a sharp watch on the Sikani that constantly bother the men, the natives always trying to get their hands on blankets, guns, flour, anything. The Indians have no success as Macdonald keeps a rotating guard posted the entire night.

Eventually they reach the Techieca. The going is easy at first across open bedrock covered sparsely with a thin carpet of lichens that are drab blue-green and washed-out orange. Then they drop down into the burned forest that stretches up into mountains as far as they can see. Charred stumps shattered at their tops stand like black skeletons as do others lying at odd, jumbled angles along the scorched earth that the intense heat of the conflagration has turned the color of dried blood, the soil exposed along the crests of wind and water-swept rises. Small green spruce and some birch, maybe a few inches tall struggle to bring back the life in this fire spawned desert. The party camps at the edge of this nightmarish landscape, near a small creek of the clearest cold water. Thick, spongy clumps of emerald moss grow along one side of the water. On the other the bank is mostly bare, blackened stone. The fire stopped here for whatever reason – rain, snow, an act of a natural god. They began crossing the wasteland at sunrise the next day, the men moving silently across the graveyard landscape. Baptiste leads the string of horses on foot. He talks softly with the animals urging them along, allaying their fears with the gentle murmuring rhythms of his voice.

"All is well my friends. No fear this day. Baptiste takes care of you in this place," and the like, over and over in the calmest of tones that are hypnotic. The horses listen and follow, hooves clattering on bare rock or kicking up small clouds of gray ash. They trust this man. Animal instinct tells them that the Frenchman will see all of them through this supernatural maze. They nicker and snort as they communicate among themselves.

The party covers the area in two days that fortunately are mostly dry with only a brief thunderstorm or squall after sunset. A steady rain would have turned the soil into a quagmire. The evening rains serve to keep the dust down somewhat during the days' marches. Much time is spent clearing the deeper deposits of ash along the new trail. Pine boughs cut by the stream before venturing into this barren ground are used as brooms. Shovels are also kept busy. Men, horses, gear, everything is soon covered with a thick, clinging gray-white, powdery ash that coats the ground a couple of inches thick despite the passing of nearly two years. The flows of small streams and the downpours of immense storms are insufficient to cleanse the land of this grime.

Finally Macdonald's group clears the burn area and starts up a wide trail that switchbacks to the Pacific-Arctic divide. Little work is needed along this stretch – some leveling, removing a downed tree here and there, pushing a boulder over the side and watching it tumble and crash into the river a thousand feet below. Progress despite the steepness of the path and the altitude is easy and swift. At the crest they stop to rest, eat some bannock and dried moose meat, make tea and enjoy the view of mountain ranges that tear up the sky in all directions. To the west a plateau of deep green pine forest stretches to the horizon. Bursting up in the middle of all of those trees like gigantic mushrooms are a group of rounded, bald mountains whose tops are covered in snow that gives way to rock colored gray-purple. North, east, south – sharp ridges of mountain summits stretch forever until lost from view by the curvature of the earth.

The sound of men approaching up the trail on the Arctic side of the divide drifts on the wind to the group. The language is clearly of some Indian dialect – animated, guttural sounds whose origins are based on living in the North Country for hundreds of generations – verbal symbols that mimic the wind swirling around mountain peaks, rushing water, avalanches racing down bare chutes, thunder. Where the Mounties are taking their lunch is sheltered by a ridge of rock that blocks the view coming up from the other side of the pass. They all stand, wondering if these natives will be friendly or hostile. Working along the last switchback is a hunting part of a dozen Tagisch Indians, most likely in search of the plentiful moose of the Techieca River valley. They are dressed in hides, furs and feathers of animals indigenous to the region – caribou, marten, beaver, eagle, even grizzly claws on necklaces. Dabs and bars of red and black color are streaked across their prominent cheeks and across their foreheads. The feathers are stuck in their hair in patterns that seem to worship chaos, large primaries of raptors and from ravens point out from their skulls at all angles. Leggings are decorated with porcupine quills arranged on geometric patterns along the shins and thighs. The Indians look up and spot the seven men and the band of horses tethered to large rocks.

The leader of the group, a tall man of dark reddish-brown complexion, dressed completely in caribou buckskin and carrying a carbine sees the members of the expedition first.

He halts dead in his tracks, eyes wide, mouth open. The others do the same. All is silence among both groups. The Tagisch stare at the gray-white visages of the Mounties and Baptiste and their ghostly grouping of horses. Then they all, as if on cue, scream in terror, loud, deep-throated wails of horror that rise in pitch and volume as the Indians flee back down the trail whooping and firing their rifles into the air in a blurred streak of native dress and color. The yelling and attendant gunfire is heard for long minutes. The men move to the edge of the trail and watch as the Tagisch race across the grass expanse next to the lake far below them and then disappear into the spruce forest. Three ravens lift off from a large pine, soaring into the sky with beating wings and wild cries. Their course mirrors that of the Tagisch. The sounds of flight diminish and finally fade away entirely. Random gunshots continue echoing among the mountain peaks.

"I think we just scared the hell out of some of the local inhabitants," said Baptiste to the other men who at first are shocked at the behavior of the Tagisch. Then as the realization that their appearance probably represented every evil deity known to these wild people, an image that surely indicated that their lives and most likely their world was at an end. All of the men began laughing, uncontrollably both at the obviously absurd picture they must present and as a release of the tension built up these past weeks along the hundreds of miles of trail they broke through some of the harshest country on the continent. "They ran like we were devils. Indeed. Perhaps we are demons."

"I believe that our reputation will precede us for the

remainder of our little adventure. The legend and power of the Northwest Mounted Police continues to grow and spread throughout the land," said Macdonald. He laughs and lights his pipe. "And that of the Metis, too. We'll make camp on the shore of the mountain tarn below us. After it is established, all of us will clean our clothing and ourselves along with the horses. I'll not have our mission known as The Ghost Patrol. Some things simply are not acceptable among decent men such as ourselves."

With that the party starts down the trail to the turquoise water of the high altitude lake, the headwaters of the Kechika River. A massive glacier drops down the flank of a mountain in the west, the ice crawling towards the green of trees, moss and grass far below. Water pours and rushes everywhere – from springs, out of caverns in the ice, down rock chutes. On this day all of the hard work and loneliness seems worthwhile. The place appears a wilderness paradise. Macdonald's group is in high spirits. They laugh and talk animatedly among themselves. Their mood is contagious. Baptiste's horses step lightly as they work down the trail towards camp. Marmots, brown furry creatures of the high rocks and cliffs, stand on furry hind legs and whistle among themselves, the high-pitched call piercing the air and bouncing off the sheer faces of the mountains. An eagle glides overhead. It's cry sharper than the marmots'. It rides the widening gyre of an afternoon thermal, the large bird eventually disappearing over a glacier tumbling down to the west.

The next month is spent carving their way through the nearly impenetrable wilderness of forest, rivers, muskeg, marshy ponds, enormous wind-blown lakes many miles long, and fording swift, deep rivers. They struggle up precipitous trails that arc over mountain summits, tracks that cling dangerously to cliffs that drop away thousands of feet to uncharted rivers far below. They shoot goats and

Faro sheep and even the marmots for the stew pot. Grass is plentiful and the horses do well, though two of them stumble and plummet down a jagged slope, perishing as they cartwheel in a series of frantic cries. The few Indians they spot from a distance flee at their approach with wild yelps and screams. The Ghost Patrol becomes a running joke with the men. Often the Mounties work in a chilled soup of water, moss and aquatic plants that is shoulder high. Mosquitoes and black flies make their labors a perpetual hell. Moose flies resembling gigantic horseflies chomp chunks of flesh from arms, scalps, faces. Macdonald drives the men hard. He knows that work is the only way to endure in this country and the only way to eventually see the task to its completion. Within weeks they reach the Liard River and stick to the shore Faille recommended. They follow the river that is more than a mile wide in places to its headwaters in the Saint Cyr Range that runs southeast to northwest in a series of treeless summits that are home to the goats and sheep who find safety on the mountain slopes.

Climbing a sharp divide, they next drop down into the Pelly River drainage, a severe valley choked with brush and forest. After weeks of struggle they reach the main river and a couple of days later the confluence of the Pelly, Ross and Lapie rivers. The weather has been unusually warm lately, in the seventies with nighttime lows of above twenty degrees. Frost covers plants, trees and gear in the mornings, but not severe.

Macdonald has a decision to make now. Should he finish the journey by land following the river and breaking trail all the way to Fort Selkirk, perhaps as much as 250 river miles and another six weeks? Or should he order his men to build stout rafts to float easily down the Pelly until it joins the Yukon at his final destination covering the distance in a matter of days?

"Sir, you've been given discretion as to deciding the most prudent and efficient way to Fort Selkirk," said Galpin. "I believe that reasonable men will follow our travel instructions and float the remaining distance. They will build their own rafts or purchase canoes from the natives in the area. It is far easier than fighting this damned forest and the muskeg. In time riverboats will work up and down this river."

"It's not the reasonable men that I'm worried about," said Macdonald. "The greedy fools too eager to consider the rational course will forgo the days needed to build a decent raft and strike off blindly into the woods. Or they may construct a craft that is slipshod, not worthy to travel the Peel. Those men's fates I hold in my hands, at least in some small way. I'm all for floating. It would be easier and save a good deal of time, but I believe that to be true to the spirit and intent of our orders we must continue to make trail. And we could never build craft to ferry the horses. We'd have to post a man with Baptiste until we returned."

The contingent, expecting that their hard labors are mostly ended, are clearly disappointed with the decision to cut another couple of hundred miles of trail. But they are Mounties and they obey their superior with no dissent or bickering. Baptiste tends to the horses without complaint. For the next five weeks the party works its way through the thickest tangles of bush and expanses of forest of the entire journey. Insects are horrendous. Grizzlies and black bears savage their food stores. Moose numbers dwindle and the men turn to snagging early running salmon that have migrated all the way upriver from the Pacific along with resident grayling and Dolly Vardon. They use spears cut from small aspen, tips sharpened to hooked points. In the feeder creeks the salmon are thick, hundreds of them, their dark, sleek backs either just below the water's surface or rising clear of the stream. The thirty-pound and larger fish are all fight as they struggle determinedly upstream to ancient spawning grounds. A couple of the larger fish pull the men into the current after them when the barb-like hook sinks into the thick muscles along their flanks. The change in diet for the men is a welcome one. The fish are easy to come by at this time of the year as they move up the rivers and creeks by the millions.

Between the three rivers' confluence and Fort Selkirk the party must make a lengthy detour to the south around a landslide over a mile wide where the face of a mountain has sheared away and millions of cubic yards of rock have rushed down into the river. The boulder field is impassable, not only for horses, but men as well. While the event may have happened hundreds of years ago, the scarred side of the mountain appears to be a recent event, natural world time being far more expansive than human existence. The Pelly's current has been shoved radically to the north side of the river channel and the large volume of water now squeezes through a rocky passage that shoots the water in a roaring tumult, whitewater swirling downstream for a half-mile. Macdonald and Galpin think that the stretch can be floated, but would require caution and extreme concentration, plus a sturdy craft.

Along the detour they encounter a geologic structure that Macdonald will label Volcano Mountain on his map. It is located immediately north of the junction of the Pelly and Yukon rivers. The volcano consists of twin-rounded cones of roughly 1,000 feet above the valley floor and a series of lava flows that issued through breaks in the cone wall both to the northeast and the southwest many centuries past. The northeastern lava flow traveled about three miles and the southwestern flows, only about one. The volcano appears to be long dormant. The lava fields are marked with dwarf birch and lodge pole along with clumps of grass and fireweed, this plant's bright flowers lighting up the otherwise bleak landscape with its warm pink-lavender blossoms. Small birds flit among the flowers hunting insects that are drawn to the scent of the blossoms. The ubiquitous marmots can be heard whistling among themselves out of sight somewhere along the higher reaches of the lava flows.

While skirting the ragged, mangled terrain the men encounter a prospector leading an old gray mule. The man is short, stooped with age and the tedious labor of washing rock samples looking for traces of gold. His clothes are worn with holes in the knees and elbows.

The old timer stops and greets the men with a "Howdy," and a wave of a gnarled, tanned hand that is missing the last two fingers. The mule snorts and paws the ground in recognition of the horses' presence. Macdonald drops off his mount and approaches the man.

"I'm Sergeant Macdonald. My men and I are working our way from Fort Edmonton, blazing trail," he said and offers his hand. "How far to Fort Selkirk if I may ask?"

"So you're the damn spooks those Tagisch told me about. You scared all hell out a them fellers. The fools think you're spirit gods come to take them from their earthly home. Last I saw they were heading as fast as their moccasins would carry them to the west," the old man said. "Fort's another few days away. Easy pickings, the trail is from here, though those damned mosquitoes are thick as North Sea fog up ahead, Seem to be hanging on late this year, despite the freezes we've gone through."

"That's good news. We've been at this since the first of May," said Macdonald. "We'll all be glad to finish our task."

"A trail for idiots I imagine," said the prospector. "None of the city slickers has any idea what it takes. Think the gold will find them. Not the other way around. Hell, I'm damn rich and could care less. It's the chase I'm seekin.' Not the infernal yellow metal, but just the same, look at this, will ya."

The old man shuffles to one of the packs attached to the

mule's flanks with diamond hitches. He unties the rope and opens the lid. He pulls out a leather-wrapped object about the size of a slightly flattened, seven-inch ball that has oblong dimensions. Whatever it is, it is heavy. The man uses both hands to carry it over to Macdonald. He sets it on the ground and pulls the stained leather covering away.

Macdonald sucks in air. He gasps. A gold nugget that must weigh twenty pounds at least sparkles in the sunlight. The appearance is that of a metallic potato with a dimpled surface. It must be worth thousands of dollars.

Picking up on Macdonald's thoughts the prospector said "Found it right around here. Man from the H.B. Company offered me $10,000 for this here nugget. I said no. And I've got more just like this one buried in the back of a cave tucked away in these mountains. If rich I was after, I'd already have caught the road for the big city. These old peaks are full of surprises and wealth. Like I said, the chase is what I'm seeking these days."

He laughs, more of a cackle, rewraps and stashes away his treasure, then picks up the mule's lead and heads off with a "Good day to you all."

The men are speechless. Thoughts of retiring from the Service and searching for gold right here dance through all of their heads. Macdonald, seeing this, shouts "Let's move on. Selkirk and duty's end awaits us."

Reluctantly all of them continue their circuitous path around the base of the volcano as they make their way back north towards the banks of the Pelly River. On the sixteenth of September they reach Fort Selkirk, hungry, exhausted and without an ounce of fat on them. Even Baptiste's horses are thinner, ribs beginning to show through scratched hides. The only injuries were to Galpin's shin when the flat side of an ax blade bounced off the bone, chipping and deeply bruising it; and when one of the men chopped off the tip of his little finger with a machete while not paying attention as he cut away pine boughs along the Finlay River. Discomforts, but far less than Macdonald anticipated when he left Fort Edmonton.

The fort, named after the fifth earl of Selkirk, is an assemblage of well-maintained squared-log structures on a high bank above the Yukon River. It is the largest community between Whitehorse and Dawson City a distance as a raven flies of three hundred miles. There is the main NWMP Headquarters with attached mess hall and barracks and nearby stables and corral. A private trader, Thomas Lord, has a large commercial compound adjacent to the post. Several other private entrepreneurs operate lesser concerns along a row of small cabins in the settlement.

Barking dogs alert the residents of the party's arrival. Rumors of the men moving towards Selkirk as they pushed through the forests and over the many ranges of mountains have been circulating in the region for weeks, carried and promulgated by trappers, Indians, traders and gold seekers that make up the informational network of the North Country. The arrival is a major event in both the brief history and contemporary affairs of the Yukon.

After proper introductions, stabling of stock, bunking of men and related tasks are attended to, the men are feted for three days and nights. Moose, caribou, salmon, vegetables from the fort's garden, kegs of whiskey and rum, four of cases of French wine traded for by Lord in exchange for two rifles, ammunition and a bag of roasted coffee beans from Ethiopia, a barrel of Irish ale – all of this and a great deal of enthusiasm goes into a celebration that becomes legendary, at least to those who attended "The Fort Selkirk Massacre" as it became known in the unofficial annals of NWMP lore.

Well before the land freezes solid for the winter, Macdonald completes his map and report. He posts these with a group of men bound for Fort Grahame before winter's lockup. They then make the run along the trail Macdonald's men have built from the fort to Edmonton in thirty days for a total time of eight weeks from Selkirk to civilization, a record by several weeks. Macdonald's future with the NWMP is secured with this incredible feat. Galpin is also promoted, to the rank of corporal and assigned to accompany the Inspector. He spends the winter learning all he can from trappers, prospectors and Indians about the land running north to the Mackenzie Delta. Orders and a notification of his promotion to inspector arrive in March he is ready to take on his new duties. Macdonald and Galpin return to Edmonton, but with the outbreak of the Boer War, Macdonald enlists as a sergeant in the 2nd Canadian Mounted Rifles in January 1900, as does Galpin with a rank of corporal. After a year of action in South Africa, the two men remain with the army through 1902 when they are discharged. Both re-enlist in the NWMP in early 1903 and are assigned to their old stomping grounds at Fort Edmonton.

~ ~ ~

The Inspector looks out beyond Pauline Cove and the whaling ships resting easily at anchor. In the distance he sees a towering bank of fog moving in on Herschel Island. This is always an indication of, at the very least, a wind-generated ice storm, usually much more than this manifesting itself in the form of lengthy blizzards powered by polar gales. He remembers his arrival at Herschel when he had to make do with a pair of squalid sod huts that he rented for $45 a month from a local whisky trader. At that time only two ships wintered in the cove, and there was only one metal building instead of the dozen now. Perhaps seventy whites spent that first cold season at the cove along with a fluctuating population of aboriginals. Today the number is more than several hundred, the number varying on the weather and whaling conditions. He recalls all of the struggles he had establishing order among the chaos and stamping out the liquor sales to the Inuits and the rest of the aboriginals; and he remembers the brutal winters, the isolation and his never-ending drive to establish a permanent, efficient NWMP post on this rocky point far beyond the edge of nowhere. He's accomplished this and wonders where his next assignment will take him. Maybe he'll learn of this when he arrives in Dawson City this winter.

"Only a matter of time," he says to the approaching weather and to Galpin.

The Corporal looks his way, then smiles.

The two men head inside to prepare for the trip to Fort McPherson.

-CHAPTER THREE-

We were under constant surveillance for any sign of inability or show of weakness that might endanger the lives of others of the patrol. So much depended on perfection.

Constable Taylor Phelps
Winter NWMP patrol
1905-1906

NJOOTLI REFUSES TO ACCOMPANY THEM on the winter run to Dawson City next week. The Loucheaux is adamant. His mind is made up. He's not angry or aggressive, but his stance – arms folded across his chest, legs spread apart, steady eye contact maintained with the other four men – indicates his resolve. They are gathered in the NWMP headquarters at Fort McPherson, grouped in front of a hearth and a warm fire. Birch logs are crackling and popping in the sparkling flames. They've already spent most of an hour right at this spot or pacing the wood floors that creak and groan under the frustrated boot steps of the Mounties. Outside a storm rages, the screeching wind blows snow that slants nearly horizontal with an invisible landscape, terrain that's been obliterated by the whiteout. Temperatures are well below zero. The sled dogs are curled up next to the iron posts they're chained to, the animals already lost beneath mounded drifts.

"I like you men very much, but the signs say don't go. Not just for me, for all of you," said Njootli. His voice is calm but filled with resolve. "Last night I heard the aurora above me very clearly. And they burned red and blue. Not good omens at all for this fellow. The devil is talking at times like this. I have never heard them so loud buzzing across this

81

land. Soft hisses in the calm of a winter's long night, but never with so much sizzle or buzzing. And when I looked again there were black lights all over the southern sky. Dark balls that moved back and forth towards where I stood. My great grandfather told me of these. When the black balls of fire mark the sky in the direction one plans to travel, there will be hunger, much cold, and death. To understand these omens you must learn to see without looking. No truth comes from staring straight at a thing, even an ignorant Loucheaux such as myself knows this much."

The other men – Inspector Macdonald and Corporal Galpin recently arrived in McPherson following an uneventful ten-day run by dog sled from Herschel Island, and Constables Fraser and McDonnell – are trying to convince the Indian to be their guide for the trip to Dawson that departs in four days on December 21st, the first official day of winter. Njootli holds his ground, shaking his head and never smiling, unheard of for him.

"No. No. No good in any way," he said. "I never go against the signs. They are warnings intended to keep me alive so I can feed my always-hungry wives. They eat worse than my disrespectful malamute sled dogs. You should not go either. The weather will be next to horrible. I can feel this in my aching knees. Lots of wind, snow and cold. Then when you may get used to all this coldness, the days will grow even colder and you'll go nowhere. Nowhere anyplace. Foolish to travel when there's good shelter and plenty of dried fish and moose meat here. You men even have your scotch whiskey that you horde among yourselves. Books to read. A good life awaits this winter. I ask you not to make this trip."

"I give up," said Macdonald. "I respect your decision, Njootli. It's yours to make. Corporal, you're to lead the way. Constables Fraser, McDonnell, and myself will prepare the sleds and provisions. You study the maps and plan our course."

"Yes sir, and I'll help with the rest, too," said Galpin, who salutes crisply and heads to a desk in back of the main office. A series of shelves hold the post's maps. He begins to search for those he needs."

Fraser turns to the Indian and tries one more time. He wants this man, his friend, to come along and guide them through the distant passes and up little-known river corridors that will be buried in many feet of snow. He has a barely realized premonition, a feeling of unease that is churning in the back of his head and in his stomach, that he and the rest of them will need all of the help and luck they can bring to bear on this trip.

"Njootli, all you have talked about this fall is that you want to get to Dawson to see your older brother and his new wife," said the Constable. "And you wanted to buy a new pair of binoculars at the mercantile. Remember? You said your eyes aren't as good as when you were 'a younger, handsome man.' And you've made the trip four times in winter already. The Inspector and Corporal have each traveled the route before. With all of that, what can go wrong? The journey's been run successfully every winter since 1904. Please reconsider."

"I'm not traveling down that way this winter," he said. "Brother has six wives. Seen one, pretty much seen them all, if you understand." He finally smiles, if only briefly. "The Inspector and Corporal make their trips the wrong damn way and later in the winter. Things are not the same when running to the south. Everything looks different, seems different, maybe damn indeed is different. The snow is different later in winter, not like it is now. No, I'll wait here and hope for your return in the spring before the snows melt and the mosquitoes come back to drive you white men crazy. That's my final say on the subject."

He nods in self-approval and walks out the front door,

the heavy wooden thing bangs shut loudly on a gust of icy wind.

"That's that," said McConnell. "We're on our own."

"Not exactly, constable," said Macdonald. "The corporal's been along the way before. And he broke trail with me from Fort Edmonton to Fort Selkirk three years ago. Twelve hundred miles through tough country. I trust this man with my life and so shall you two."

"If I may offer several suggestions, sir," said Fraser. "Instead of three sleds, I think we should load four. And I think we should add two more men. That will gives us two to break trail and one of those can carry a rifle well ahead of the dogs that may alert or spook any game ahead of us. This will increase our chances of success when it comes to acquiring fresh meat. And we should use seven dogs each. Not the usual five or six per sled. Our malamutes and Mackenzie River mixed breeds will work well at seven. The combination of malamute, husky and even wolf seems to create an animal that is strong, resilient and, in its own way, loyal. This slight change would seem advisable. We can carry more supplies and extra rifles and ammunition, even when factoring in the increased amount of food for the dogs that we'll require. And if one or two sleds break down or something happens to several of the dogs, we'll have the option of combining loads and teams."

"I'll consider this, constable," said Macdonald as he relights his pipe for the tenth or eleventh time during the afternoon's difficult meeting. "I'll give you my decision in the morning, but I think that I prefer to have just one man free at all times. He should be able to break trail, keep a constant eye out for game, and on our bearings and our progress. In this cold, if he works far enough ahead of the main party the frost will have time to set and firm up the path. I've always believed that when you can hear the leather bindings creaking of the man who is breaking, either is moving too slowly or those behind are not giving him ample room to do his work properly. Travel light and travel accurately. That seems to make sense."

The meeting's over. The men separate and attend to their respective duties.

After looking at the maps, some of them reasonably current and therefore helpful because of the annual excursions by the NWMP between Fort McPherson and Dawson City, Galpin breaks the journey down into sixteen sections based on geography. The routes taken by past patrols are drawn in. Much of these maps are blank, areas where either no one has traveled and or has made measurements or drawings to plot the topography. On either side of the NWMP patrol route from the junction of the Peel and Wind rivers to Hart Pass in the Wernecke's on the eastern edge of the Blackstone Plateau, most of the territory is empty, blank or with the word "uncharted." He marks the sections on the appropriate maps. Among them are stretches that run from the post along and over the Peel River for seventy miles, forty-nine miles up the Wind River, fifty-four more up the Little Wind, ten across the Wind-Hart Divide in the Wernecke Mountains, and the easy pitches at the end for sixty-four miles down Twelvemile River and eighteen into Dawson City.

Macdonald comes over and looks at the maps, noticing the empty areas.

"We'll see what we can do to fill in some of those areas," he said. "If the weather allows us, I think we can add greatly to the knowledge of the land along our route, something to help future patrols, eh, Corporal?"

"Yes we can, sir," said Galpin. "Much like we did when we blazed trail from Edmonton. I took a good deal of satisfaction in that particular work."

Four days later, time that seemed to pass all too quickly for everyone, all was in readiness. Orders for the Mounties remaining at the fort have been discussed at length and also posted on a bulletin board in headquarters. These are to be carried out until the men return sometime in late March or early April.

Among the hundreds of pounds of supplies packed away for the trip that is expected to take approximately one month are: one-thousand pounds of dried fish for the dogs, thirty-pounds of tobacco, twenty pounds of candles, and about ninety pounds of food per man. Macdonald is counting on killing game such as moose and caribou along the way to augment this and possibly trading with Loucheaux hunting parties that are often out seeking meat at this time of year. MWMP vouchers will be used for this purpose and the Indians can redeem them at the Hudson Bay store at McPherson or other ones located about the region. Provisions for the men include one hundred-twenty pounds of flour, fifteen pounds of lard, ten of butter, eight of bacon, ten of corned beef, twenty of tinned milk, twenty of dried apples, currants and apricots, thirty of beans, thirty-five of sugar, eighteen of coffee and tea and six pounds of baking powder. Salt and pepper are included. There is also a one-gallon cask of Cardhu single-malt scotch whiskey to be distributed in modest rations measured out after a particularly productive day on the trail. Macdonald rarely includes liquor on assignments, but has found that when used modestly at appropriate times the communal aspects of a drink shared around an evening's fire is an excellent way to boost or maintain morale. He's saved this cask since it was delivered to him by a whaler last summer, the whiskey coming all the way from the Highlands of Scotland west of Dufftown. The distillery is located near the headwaters of his favorite Atlantic salmon river. Also included are down-filled sleeping bags, a Yukon stove, tarps used as tents and to protect supplies, cooking utensils, two large axes, a pair of hand axes, pocket barometer, thermometer and sextant, personal gear including clothing, watches, matches and the group's only weapon, a Winchester Model 94 .30-30 carbine and four boxes of ammunition.

The eight-foot, 16-inch wide, ash- and pine-wood sleds are loaded to their maximum carrying capacity and then covered with the tarps that are secured by hemp ropes. The ash runners are covered with two inches of iron plating. This retards wear when traveling over rocky stretches and also glides across and through the snow better than bare wood. The sleds weigh nearly eighty pounds unloaded. The sled is guided through tight places with a gee-pole that extends from the front of the sled on the right or gee. It is about six feet long, three inches thick and extends to the musher's shoulder. Often the sleds are guided from the rear by a man shifting his weight from one side or the other and even dragging a foot to direct the course of the team. The men make sparing use of twenty-five-foot whips that are made from plaited seal hide to control the animals beginning with the first dog in line called a wheeler or wheel dog. The term comes from horses pulling wagons where the first animal or animals in harness were closest to the wagon's wheels. The whips are only used to strike dogs that are fighting among them selves, otherwise the sharp noise inches above their heads is sufficient.

Macdonald vetoes the additional sled Fraser suggested, but does up the number of dogs in each set of traces to seven. The malamutes and Mackenzie River breeds tug at their harnesses. They moan, growl and bark in their eagerness. All except Wraith. He remains silent, alert, watching all that is going on around him. They are ready to begin. The other dogs are big, too, between eighty and one hundred-thirty pounds. While the men take good care of the animals and are always alert to their needs and any injuries they may suffer along the trail, these sled dogs are not pets and they are not treated as such. They are handled with respect and dealt with in a fair but stern disciplined way. The dog teams are looked on almost as living machines that can mean the difference between life and death when traveling in wilderness that is hundreds of miles from the nearest man-made shelter. For the past three weeks Fraser, McConnell and the other constables have run the animals as much as twenty miles a day in an attempt to round them into trail condition. The snow was already more than six feet of packed powder with a lighter covering of about a foot that fell the night before last.

Njootli is nowhere to be seen. In fact, no one's sighted the Loucheaux since the day of the meeting at headquarters. Even his wives have no idea where he's gone. Perhaps to an isolated fishing shack he keeps a few miles down the Peel. But one thing's for certain, Njootli is having absolutely nothing to do with this patrol. He's left four pairs of hand carved goggles for the men. These are made from the outer layer of caribou horn with intricate designs of caribou and moose on them. They are held in place with leather straps. Slits are cut into them, but most of the potentially blinding light is blocked. Snow blindness is a painful and debilitating condition that can waylay a party for days, and is to be avoided if at all possible. The men admire Njootli's workmanship. They appreciate his thoughtful gifts that are far superior to the goggles they've made on their own.

Finally on the shortest day of the year and near the phase of a new moon, the first official day of winter according to the calendar, with Macdonald manning the lead, they head out amid yells of "Mush," "So long," "Good luck" and the excited cacophony of the baying dogs. Many Loucheaux, a band of Inuits down from the Beaufort ice, trappers, and a lone prospector recently come in from his mountain valley claim for the winter stand on the snow-covered parade ground in front of headquarters. All of them cheer and wave and wish the patrol good luck. This is a major event in the life of the post. Even if everything goes as planned, a touch of good fortune can't hurt, especially in the unforgiving environment of an Arctic winter.

Galpin, wearing snowshoes that are a compromise between the wide oval used for deep powder and the elongated shape designed for forest travel, begins breaking trail. The shoes are of his own design based on many winters' experience in this land. Wraith Dhogge is at the head of the string, the enormous, lengthy Irish hound pulling easily in his traces. Clouds of breath rise from his jaws and nostrils. The mist trails behind him like exhaust from a steam engine. The Inspector had hoped that trappers and hunters would have already accomplished Galpin's job for him during the first seventy miles of the trip, but no one has been moving through the drainage in the uncommonly harsh weather of the past week. The snow is expected, but the constant winds whipping down from the mountains in the southeast are unusual for this time of year. Here is one of the first differences from traveling north to south. Had they been coming from the other direction the trail would have been well established for the first eighty miles or more heading out of Dawson. And a horse and sled is often used to further improve the trail for the initial fifty miles. This allows both dogs and men to get their "trail legs" before tackling the rigors of unbroken trail. Even with these difficulties, the buildings of Fort McPherson are soon out of sight behind the low rolling swales.

While all of the dogs are seasoned travelers in the wilderness, the canines' diverse personalities need constant care and discipline in order to at least create a semblance of order. Some dogs are passive and submissive, while others are dominant and constantly assert themselves. Wraith reigns supreme, his superiority established through a series of often bloody and deadly battles with other dogs who sought to be the leader or alpha male. The fights were over in seconds with the hound always the clear victor. He is left alone. The men don't chain him up at night like the others. There's no need. Wraith keeps to himself. The dogs are harnessed in a hitch – walked into their collars with the traces on either side of them. The first dog is called the wheel, and the succeeding are numbered six, five, four, three, two and the lead. Unlike Eskimo setups where the dogs are each tied to a separate line and fan out to pull the sled, Mountie sleds have the dogs pull inline to facilitate slipping between the tight spaces found in forests and in negotiating the narrow, exposed mountain trails. There are times when certain animals dislike each other and will take advantage of any opportunity to fight. The handler must be aware of this and do his best to keep the antagonists separated, even at times when the sled has upset and all is free-form madness for some time. An injured dog is normally turned out of the team until the wound heals, making more work for the others, a situation to be avoided in the delicate balance between progress and failure. Mean dogs are culled from the pack back at the fort. There is no time to work with this type of disposition on the trail. And all injuries from dogfights must be eliminated or reduced as much as possible to avoid delays or worse.

The sleds don't have handles on them so the men must guide them with ropes attached to the frames. Sometimes when moving down a slope speeds reach fifteen miles-per-hour. The Mounties must stand on the backs of the runners, at best a tenuous position, as the outfits sail through the countryside. Galpin hurries to the side at these moments allowing the others to pass and then does his best to catch up in as short a time as possible. The trailbreaker is exhausted by evening. The job rotates on a daily basis with even the Inspector taking his turn, though the Corporal insists on two days straight during his stint. Macdonald agrees. The Inspector believes in chain of command and discipline, but he leads by allowing men to express themselves and participate in the decision making process. If he feels that an idea or suggestion has merit he makes the appropriate changes.

Because of the tough trail conditions, the men only cover fifteen miles the first day. While the Inspector had hoped for twenty-five, this average will mean the completion of the patrol in one month. He expects to make much better time once they reach the Blackstone River Valley and the run to Dawson along trail that is mostly downhill through good snow.

At the first night's camp the dogs are released from their harnesses and chained to trees far enough apart so none of them can reach each other in order to avoid fights over food or because of conflicting temperaments. Poles are cut for "pitching the fly" or raising the tents, spruce bows laid for the floors, two logs cut and trimmed to be used as a base for the stove and firewood gathered. All of the dogs' feet are examined for cuts, clumps of snow and for ice chunks wedged in their paws. Sled runners are also cleaned of ice, snowshoes repaired if need be and ice is chopped from the Peel for cooking. Tea or coffee is prepared immediately. The role of cook rotates, but often evolves to the man who can prepare food the best and may actually prefer the chore. That first night each Mountie picks a place in his tent, one that he will keep for the duration of the journey. Macdonald and Galpin share one tent while Fraser and McConnell share the other. This entire routine is reversed in the morning, but is usually more difficult because the temperature is lower than at the end of the previous day and the men's movements are sluggish from the night's inactivity. This pattern will continue with only slight variations over the course of the patrol.

That night Macdonald writes down the day's events in his logbook. He then reads over some comments from previous patrols, observations he has written down in another notebook. These include the 1906-07 run that included Galpin:

31st Dec. 1906, left camp at 8:30; traveled to head of creek and crossed over the divide into a creek running into the Little Wind River. These divides are very low.

1st January, '07, left camp at 7:30; traveled down the creek to the Little Wind River, and down the river for about two miles and camped.

2nd, left camp at 8:00 a.m.; continued on down the Little Wind; had a hard time on the glaciers today, the ice being so smooth and the wind so high that it was almost impossible for men and dogs to travel.

3rd, left camp at 8:30: make mouth of Little Wind River, about 25 miles and camped.

"I don't see a problem with this or the rest of any of it," said Macdonald to Galpin who is looking at a map covering tomorrow's route. "You'll see us through, eh, Corporal. The dogs are fit. Constables Fraser and McConnell are good men. We've plenty of food and will surely find game along the way. I hope to reach the portage cutoff up the Trail River that crosses the headwaters of the Caribou by day after next. The portage will save us close to two days travel, but it's not the clearest track to locate is it corporal?"

"I'm not concerned. Even if we take one of the lesser forks we'll still reach the Peel and manage to save at least a day. But I'll locate the correct cutoff. We're in good shape, sir," said Galpin. "We'll get there."

With that, the Inspector blows out the candle, climbs well into his bag and falls asleep.

The men are on the trail before dawn. The days are short with only a few hours of daylight that even on sunny days is subdued and not filled with the brilliance of the summer sun. At noon there is a twilight feel to the landscape. Shadows are tinted with slight purple. Silence dominates the land, except for the wind that pours down from the high country. The overall luminance is subdued, muted.

At this hour stars, galaxies and the remains of a crescent moon dropping down over the southwest horizon compete with the ever-present northern lights flashing brilliantly overhead. The weather is now ideal for travel. The temperature is minus fifteen, making the snow hard and crisp providing an excellent surface for both dogs and sled runners. A lone raven glides downstream in the direction of Fort McPherson. Shortly thereafter an eagle follows the same course only much higher above the river. They cover nearly six miles during the first two hours. The sun has risen and shows itself as a glowing silver-yellow orb that seems to be having second thoughts about climbing much higher above the distant horizon. The men are in good spirits. Galpin leads the way and sets a strong pace as he breaks trail through the fresh snow. His enthusiasm is contagious and carries over to even the dogs. Wraith lets loose one of his rare howls as they round a bend in the river and spot a moose standing on the ice. Macdonald grabs the rifle and fires three times at the motionless animal. He misses low and to the right, the errant bullets kick up tufts of snow in front of the moose. Then it dashes for the far bank and the sheltering forest and is gone. The echoes of the gunfire return from the rising slopes of mountain foothills south of the party. The group stays close to the high cut bank overlooking the Peel. They manage to skirt the forest that grows to within thirty or forty feet of the edge before petering out. A few trees cling to the soil along this open stretch of land, some of them tilted at gravity-defying angles out over the frozen river, their roots exposed. They'll be washed away in next spring's runoff.

The patrol climbs a long, gradual rise for the next couple of miles. They stop and have a meal of bannock, dried caribou, dried apples and tea. The dogs are given a ration of fish. Then the group sets out once more, this time on an easy glide as the course takes them from several hundred feet above the Peel to only twenty. Macdonald and the others, except Galpin, climb onto the back edges of the runners and enjoy the ride with only occasional sharp commands to the dogs that seem happy to be out on the trail this day.

Macdonald revels in the enormous, empty landscape and the sound of the sled runners whispering through the snow, the images of men and dogs working together in the complete whiteness of an Arctic winter. He takes pride in being part in an organization that has done so much over the years to bring law and order to the Canadian Northwest. This patrol is one more example of the Mounties' presence in the region. Over the last four-plus decades the NWMP has built a strong reputation based on fairness, discipline, swift and decisive action, and attention to duty that commands respect of all – white and Indian alike. Few men argue with a Mountie's judgment. Men that have crossed paths with them are quickly disabused of their recalcitrant notions. If not, they find themselves imprisoned or dead. Their word is law in the north country. This respect was hard earned over the years.

All of this began when The Canadian Confederation in 1867 brought the region of the Northwest under control of the Dominion of Canada. The gradual withdrawal of the Hudson's Bay Company from a number of river drainages, a commercial entity that had at least the illusion of stability in the region during the previous two hundred years, resulted in the introduction of a destructive new threat in the form of the American whiskey trade. Traders would run back and forth across the U.S.-Canada border that was essentially a no-man's land. They would drive wagons carrying barrels of whiskey that they sold for enormous profit then they'd retreat to the safety of the States, most often in Montana and to a lesser extent in North Dakota. The whiskey men were rough trade. Killing was nothing to them. Ruining the native way of life by alcoholism meant nothing. Drunken debauches, violence, rape of native women, murder were all commonplace along the lawless frontier of the border. What few laws were in place appeared made to be broken. On May 3, 1873, Sir John A. MacDonald, no relation to the Inspector, introduced a bill into Parliament that sought to bring order to the region, and also to encourage settlement, and establish Canadian authority in the Northwest Territories. The Bill was passed seventeen days later, creating the Northwest Mounted Police. Two contingents, totaling close to four hundred men were recruited and trained, uniting at Fort Dufferin, Manitoba in June, 1874.

The group marched west. After two months of fighting the intense sun, extreme heat and marauding thunderstorms packing wind, lightning and hail, the contingent finally reached the Milk River Ridge, where they encamped and awaited provisions contracted by the Mountie's Assistant Commissioner, James Farqueson Macleod in Fort Benton, Montana. With winter's imminent approach, a guide, Jerry Potts, was obtained to assist Macleod in quickly establishing a presence in the southern territory. Potts led Macleod and the remaining NWMP members to the notorious whisky post, Fort Whoop-Up. When the North-West Mounted Police arrived at the site, they found the post abandoned except for one lone caretaker, and dozens of empty whiskey casks. They were able to build their permanent post before winter. This fort, built on an island in the Old Man River west of Fort Whoop-Up, was named Fort Macleod after the assistant commissioner.

On July 8, 1874, two hundred-seventy-five officers and enlisted men of the Northwest Mounted Police, along with one hundred-forty-two draught oxen, ninety-three head of cattle, three-hundred-ten horses, one hundred-fourteen Red River carts, seventy-three wagons, two nine-pounder field guns, two mortars, mowing machines, portable forges and field kitchens, began their trek from Fort Dufferin, Manitoba to establish order in the Canadian west. The Mounties never did anything halfway. All or nothing as this fast-moving strike force meant to show any outlaws or potential lawbreakers in the region. Following the Boundary Trail, the men traveled into the territory now known as the Canadian province of Saskatchewan, where a group was dispatched Northwest to establish a post near Fort Edmonton. The bulk of the men continued west.

In addition to fighting the whiskey trade, the NWMP came to secure peaceful relations with the Indian tribes of the Canadian plains. Treaties were signed with both the Cree and Blackfeet including the Blood and Pigean bands, in 1876 and 1877. This was key to settling the region as the Blackfeet had established a reputation as fierce fighters often referred to as "raiders of the northern plains." They were skilled horsemen and fearless warriors that struck terror into all that encountered, had encountered or had only heard tales of their fighting abilities.

Four thousand workingmen poured into the Canadian west between 1882 and 1885 to build the Canadian Pacific Railway. The NWMP stationed a few of its five hundred members at each construction camp to keep illegal liquor, horse stealing, and strikes to a minimum. The Mounties also calmed the various bands of Indians who feared the changes that the "iron horse" would bring. The huge metal engines with their bellowing smoke and steam, piercing whistles and raucous piston sounds seemed like the end of the world to the Indians. The diplomacy involved in easing the situation was subtle and sophisticated involving an awareness of Indian cultural and spiritual nuance coupled with an awareness of trade goods that the native people desired. Because of the Mounties firm but fair handling of the many problems and disputes that arose during this period, amazingly few serious crimes were committed during construction. The completion of the railroad in 1885 resulted in a watershed of new settlement into western Canada. As a result, a system of patrols and outposts was established to deal with the influx of new settlers.

The desire by the Canadian government and the NWMP to establish peaceful settlement of the west was disrupted in 1885. Frustrated by the lack of responsiveness to their complaints, some Metis and Indian bands reacted violently against authority, leading to what has become known as the North-West Rebellion. The first shots of this uprising were fired at Duck Lake, on March 26, 1885. The newly completed Canadian Pacific Railway transported a military force, under the direction of Major-General Middleton, which put an end to the rebellion. The Metis and Indians were both intimidated and overwhelmed by the Mounties' show of strength. The so-called rebellion ended quickly.

The rush for gold in the Klondike region of the Yukon created a new challenge for the NWMP. While the Mounties created a presence in the territory in 1895, the Mountie contingent in the Yukon grew from nineteen men to two hundred eighty-five at the height of the Gold Rush in 1898 to ensure that law and order was maintained. Macdonald's famous trail-breaking expedition from Edmonton to Fort Selkirk on the Yukon River not only furthered the NWMP presence in the area, it gave officials back in Ottawa impetus and leverage to pass legislation that extended the Mounties' authority and powers of discretion regarding mining claim and other property disputes.

Establishment of law and order, similar to settlement of the prairies, preceded the opening up of Canada's Arctic frontier. Although attention was focused upon the Mounted Police's significant role in the Yukon, it had already begun to extend enforcement activities into the sub-Arctic forests of Canada's middle north – the Athabasca country, the Mackenzie River system and the Keewatin District west of Hudson's Bay. By the end of the nineteenth century, traders, trappers and prospectors frequently roamed these areas in search of the natural resources that were abundant in the area. As a result there was a growing need for more effective control to protect the native people from white predation, enforce liquor laws and administer hunting regulations.

A patrol had been made to York Factory on Hudson's Bay as early as 1890. Another patrol three years later extended the Force's influence into the Athabasca country. In 1897, Inspector A.M. Jarvis and two men reached Fort Resolution on Great Slave Lake and later that year permanent detachments were established at Fort Chipewyan, Athabasca Landing and Lesser Slave Lake.

Because men were needed to police the gold rush, the movement to establish authority northward was slowed. It did not pick up until Yukon conditions began to stabilize. Through a detachment and patrol network, the Mounties gradually extended their authority throughout the band of boreal forest to the Arctic Ocean's barren shores.

In 1903 a dispute between Canada and the United States over the Alaskan boundary location prompts a new thrust northward. The judicial council arbitrating the case decided in favor of the American claim. Ottawa became concerned that American whalers' activities along Canada's Arctic coasts might lead to further territorial loss. As a result Superintendent Hay ordered Macdonald and four Constables to proceed to Fort McPherson to explore the need for Western Arctic posts. Macdonald acquired detachment quarters from the local mission. His initial visit to the region laid the groundwork for the post that Fraser and McConnell are assigned to several years later. The next few years saw him complete a number of similar assignments in both the Yukon and Northwest Territories. The Inspector earned the reputation of being a man who was able to solve disputes and extend the NWMP's influence regardless of the situation and its difficulties.

Thousands of miles away, on the other side of the country, Supt. J.D. Moodie and a 16-man party were preparing to leave Halifax on the S.S. "Neptune" for Hudson's Bay. Moodie's task was to police the whalers using the area and establish a post from which to extend Canadian authority westward into the Keewatin District. Fullerton was chosen as the site for a new post on the west coast of Hudson's Bay facing the southern tip of Southhampton Island. Its harbor was a frequent wintering spot for whaling vessels. Moodie and his party arrived at Fullerton on September 23, 1903, unloaded their supplies and hastened to erect detachment buildings before freeze-up. During the winter one of the men went insane, and in the cramped quarters his sickness was a great strain on the others' nerves.

In the summer of 1904, Moodie left three men behind and returned eastward on the "Neptune" to report his findings to Ottawa. He returned immediately with reinforcements and orders to extend his activities throughout the entire Hudson's Bay region, now designated "M" Division. On September 17, 1904, his party sailed from Québec City on the C.G.S. "Arctic" commanded by Captain J.E. Bernier. During the second winter at Fullerton, Moodie sent out several patrols including a mail run to Churchill and back, a distance of some 1,100 miles.

To extend control over the area covered by these two

new divisions, the NWMP began operating a system of regular winter dog team patrols. On December 27, 1904, Constable H.G. Mapley, with two other Constables and a guide, undertook a mail patrol from Dawson and, discovering a short route through the mountain ranges, reached Fort McPherson on February 2, 1905, covering the 475 miles in just over a month. In February 1906, Constable L.E. Seller inspected whaling operations in Repulse Bay and Lyon's Inlet, more than 500 miles north of Fullerton. Macdonald's posting at Herschel Island was not far behind.

The most spectacular patrol of this period was led by Inspector E.A. Pelletier. This young French-Canadian officer was given the task of establishing a link between "N" and "M" Divisions through almost unknown country east of Great Slave Lake. With a corporal and two Constables, Pelletier left Athabasca Landing in June 1908. Traveling by Hudson's Bay boat, the party crossed Lake Athabasca and continued down the Slave River to Fort Smith. Here they transferred to two canoes, and with three months supply of food, began the long and difficult journey eastward.

Their route took them across Great Slave Lake, over the height of land and down the Hanbury and Thelon Rivers to Baker Lake. They traversed scores of portages and were constantly attacked by hordes of insects. Pelletier reported seeing musk ox and vast herds of migrating caribou. The first part of their journey ended at Chesterfield Inlet on August 31, 1908, when they were met by a whale boat sent from Fullerton. Later that winter, Pelletier continued southward by dog team to Churchill, Norway House, and Gimli, completing a patrol of over 3,000 miles.

These and many other achievements are among the reasons why the Mounties are able to control the Northwest with an iron grip, with unquestioned authority. The NWMP doesn't have an honor roll or a decoration for distinguished service in the field. It is characteristic of them that this is the way things are within the service. They don't boast of what they've done. They don't seek publicity. It's just another day's work. And that is why Macdonald believes fervently in the necessity of successfully completing this run to Dawson City. Delivering the mail and dispatches is important, but maintaining an awareness among both whites and aboriginals that the Mounties operate as ordered on a well-defined schedule is far more significant in terms of preserving law and order in the Arctic north.

They reach a small, ice-bound tributary of the Caribou River. A miniature log cabin perched on twelve-foot stilts is visible in an opening between the spruce trees. This is a cache built three autumns back by the Mounties as a slight hedge against running out of food or other supplies while on the run to Dawson City. On the other side of the Wernecke Mountains along Twelvemile Creek sits another cache with fish, dried meat, bannock and barley flour. The food stores are a result of previous patrols and their experiences where at times rations reached low levels. Fifty pounds of fish are stored at the Caribou cache to replenish the meat already consumed by the dogs. The stilts keep wild animals like bears and wolverines from raiding the hut's contents. Deep scratches on the poles indicate that at least one wolverine got wind of the heady situation above him. The marks extend nearly six feet up above the four feet of snow on the ground. A ladder with rungs spaced far apart leads to the locked door. The men retrieve the fish and also find something else, a six-ounce tin of Rattray's Black Mallorey pipe tobacco, an exotic and welcome treat to be savored in the coming days, an unexpected luxury.

The tracks of many moose have formed a well-packed trail leading from the hilly forest that stretches off to the east, down to and across both the Caribou and Pell rivers. This finding reassures Macdonald that they will have little trouble shooting game along the trail on this side of the mountains. He has no concerns about the availability of fresh meat once they reach the Blackstone Plateau. Thousands upon thousands of the Porcupine caribou herd winter in this vast expanse lying between the Olgilvie and Tombstone Mountains. And the numbers of moose are high there, also. Wolves bring down the animals at a steady rate, but these are mainly the weaker or ill members of the herd, so, if anything, the predators are doing the caribou a service.

Off to one side of the trail a patch of snow is disturbed flecked with blood. Pieces of fluffy white fur from a snowshoe hare are scattered about the site. Larger tracks of a lynx lead away from the kill. Drag marks indicate that the cat has dragged his prey to a hiding place where it can be consumed in safety. Lynx and the hares are a fluctuating but constant dynamic in this country. When the snowshoe hare population explodes in a predictable cycle covering several years, the number of lynx increases proportionately. When numbers of the prey drop so do those of the cats. This is the way of all wilderness populations, one that men living in these regions factor into their plans if they are to survive.

The blue sky disappears behind a layer of dark-gray clouds that are sliding quickly down south from the Beaufort Sea, no doubt bringing a frozen mist, possibly heavy snow, and certainly lower temperatures right behind them. Mountain chickadees flit from tree limb to tree limb chattering among themselves as though nothing wrong will ever come their way. The patrol's already covered sixteen miles. The campsite that Macdonald has in mind along the Road River is at least eight miles distant. The location is out of the wind, near water or in this case ice and has plenty of wood for cooking and a fire. The sun is already setting over the southwestern horizon, a washed-out yellow glow marks its departure. The air smells clean, washed of any scent except that of the approaching weather's precipitation.

"Men, we've at least three more hours until we reach camp at the Road," said Macdonald. "More likely four with this thick snow. We can make it and cheat the weather tonight that's coming down on us. Put your backs into it. There's whiskey and fine tobacco ahead of us this night."

Amid a flurry of yells and exhortations to the dogs, they break free of the forest and glide along an exposed flat along the bank of the stream. Then they drop down quickly to the creek's frozen surface in a rush of churning dogs' legs and sprays of snow. The teams race up a steep track made by the moose that angles across the far slope, man and dog pushing and pulling for all their worth with loud grunts and huffs as all them crest the incline reaching a long, wide bench where the surface is unencumbered by deadfalls, brush or boulders, but as the Inspector said, the rough snow pack impedes their progress. The dogs labor to make time pulling the weighty sleds, the clinging snow of previous moisture-heavy falls clinging to runners, snowshoes and paws. Wraith sets the pace never showing any sign of fatigue as his long legs and enormous paws chew up the yards of trail. Galpin has traded places with Fraser, who was manning the third sled, but now breaks trail with a freshness that has temporarily left the Corporal who welcomes the opportunity to regroup while riding on the sled's runners.

Along the way they spot ptarmigan and spruce grouse. Fraser shots four of them and even brings down a blue grouse that was sitting on a tree limb. The Blues normally roam the higher country, but the approaching bad weather has driven it to the valley.

As Macdonald predicted, the patrol makes camp at Road River four hours later in the dark, the sun and its lingering afterglow long gone. Dogs are attended to, a fire built and camp squared away as the wind begins to pick up from the north in a determined rush through the pines. The temperature begins to drop. Snow starts falling, but the men and dogs pay this little attention. The animals are busy wolfing down their rations of fish. The men are busy with chores and stoking a roaring bonfire. Following a dinner of moose stew with some chopped carrots and potatoes, a luxury sneaked into the larder by McConnell, some dried currents gathered this fall, and several mugs of stout tea, Macdonald passes around the tin of the eagerly anticipated tobacco. He taps the wooden cask carefully and pours a healthy measure of the whiskey into each man's proffered metal mug.

"Here's to a good day's work, miles well traveled with vigorous dogs and most of all, to men who understand duty and the pleasures of a winter's trail," said Macdonald as he raises his mug in the air towards the fire and then to the other three men.

As he does this, from all directions the baying of wolves, celebrating the quarter-moon clearing the horizon and soaring up into the night sky loaded with the stars, booms and washes over the camp in waves of feral sound. The packs seem to be communicating among themselves as first a group behind the men yowls followed by another, then another, continuing in a circular pattern from north to east to south, that repeats itself before stopping entirely. Then all of the wolves howl at once, a wild sound when mixed with that of the wind and the falling snow. Now they are silent.

The men listen but hear no more sounds from the animals. All of them raise their mugs and drink some of the whiskey. The wolves' presence is palpable, the first true recognition for the men that they are now alone traveling through the wilderness in the winter. This is a sobering realization, but one they have all experienced many times before during their duty above the Arctic Circle. By the time they've finished packing, tamping and lighting their pipes, a space of a couple of minutes, the mood has passed and conversation resumes, revolving around the day's efforts and tomorrow's route. The fire burns brightly shooting orange sparks into the night, moments of light that are quickly snagged by the wind and washed to the south as the snow becomes heavy. The men's spirits are high. The dogs are bedded down and quiet. All seems well this December night.

After the others are asleep, Macdonald rolls over and looks off beyond the embers of the dying fire. He is warm, comfortable, and relaxed in his bedding. In the distance the trees appear a shade darker than the surrounding night. Beyond them the dim shapes of mountains show themselves rising far above the river corridor. The stillness along the sounds of the settling coals is peaceful. He'd forgotten how much he enjoys camping out in wild country, especially when there's a thick blanket of snow on the ground. Soon he's fast asleep.

The snow is still falling when the men prepare for the trail the next morning. A foot-and-half has accumulated so far. The dogs are nothing more than barely discernable mounds of fresh white. The temperature is minus thirty-six. It is still dark. Sunrise, such as it is at this time of year, is a few hours away. With the sounds of the fire and the smells from the cooking food the dogs awake, bursting forth from their burrows in small-scale explosions of white powder. They stretch their legs and arch their backs most of them make groaning sounds as they work out the kinks in muscles stiffened from a night's sleep. Tails wag as they see Fraser and Galpin pulling dried fish from the stores on the sleds. The camp is soon awash with the noise of twenty-one hungry dogs barking, mewling and chomping on food.

They push determinedly all day, but fail to reach Trail River. The men are forced to camp on the edge of some tightly-clumped dog fir pines, skinny little trees that grow so close together they resemble the hair on a hound. Firewood consists of chopped up trunks of the trees and piles of flimsy downfall. They attend to chores, build a fire, eat and turn in early. This has been nothing more than a workmanlike day on the trail.

About two hours after heading out on the fourth day from McPherson, December 24th, Christmas Eve, they reach Trail River and head west and upstream along the northern bank. Their course takes them through open stands of larger spruce and some birch. The forest is more open here. Not hemmed in and claustrophobic. They see fresh moose tracks along the way, but no animals. The men constantly spot wolves in groups of two and three on the either side of the trail, but they disappear like phantoms whenever the men halt the sleds. It is uncommon to see them so close to men in the middle of the day. This unusual behavior sets the men to thinking and talking among themselves whenever they stop. A little past six p.m. Macdonald halts the group on a rise next to a band of forest that overlooks the ice-bound river. He estimates that the portage cutoff is, at most, a dozen miles distant, so he decides to set up camp here and start out closer to dawn tomorrow. The later departure will ensure that Galpin has adequate daylight to locate the trail that cuts across the expanse of an enormous oxbow in the Peel River passing over the upper Caribou and terminating at Mountain Creek Cabin. The day has been a difficult go of it, spent slogging through fresh snow heavy with moisture from the sea and snaking the sleds through narrow gaps in the trees. The men are tired but in good moods due in large part to the excellent progress they are now making. With serious effort and a bit of luck they'll be at the cabin on the 27th.

"We turn here Inspector," said Galpin as he stands in the untrammeled snow ahead of the men and dogs after three hours travel the following day. Christmas, but this scarcely registers with the patrol. Proceeding with their assignment is paramount and overshadows even this holiday, though they exchange "Merry Christmas's" with each other over morning coffee. "There's Caribou Born Mountain due south of us and we move along the northern side of that series of foothills until we reach the upper portion of the Caribou River. We're a few miles below the Arctic Circle now."

Macdonald unpacks his Ramsden sextant (actually it's a pentant because it represents one-fifth of a circle instead of the more common one-sixth that most individuals use. The jewel-like instrument was made more than a century earlier by Englishman Jesse Ramsden. It was given to him by his grandfather on his tenth birthday), sights in on the dim sun and confirms the corporal's statement.

His compass is an inaccurate instrument in these northern latitudes because of wild fluctuations in where true north actually is. Using the compass to plot one's course on a map in the Arctic can be misleading, often resulting in miscalculations that can cause a person to stray far from his intended path, a potentially deadly error in this country.

The Earth's magnetic field is shaped approximately like that of a bar magnet and, like a magnet, it has two magnetic poles, one in the Canadian Arctic, referred to as the North Magnetic Pole, and one off the coast of Antarctica, due south of Australia, referred to as the South Magnetic Pole. At the North Magnetic Pole the Earth's magnetic field is directed vertically downward relative to the Earth's surface. Consequently, magnetic dip, or inclination is 90°. The North Magnetic Pole is slowly drifting across the Canadian Arctic. This pulls the compass's needle away from true north often by many degrees either east or west depending on an individual's location. Factoring in this distortion or declination is extremely difficult as it varies, often dramatically, as a person travels about the north country. As an example, if a pair of rivers merge at approximately the same location along a larger river, and both of them come in from similar directions, a compass would be of no use in determining the exact direction of flow for each stream. And if one of them offers the correct path to a given destination, a compass can't provide an accurate fix to make this selection without a determination of declination for the location where the rivers meet. This information is unavailable to the Mounties.

A sextant will give a location on the planet, but lacking an accurate map, the information is not of much use to travels such as Macdonald's patrol is undertaking. There is no way to plot the information relative to a known landmark such as a mountain peak, since no such object has yet been marked on the map. In essence, the patrol is traveling on a risky cocktail mixed from equal parts hearsay, slight experience, intuition and luck.

Macdonald's sightings also tend to confirm that Caribou Born is directly south of the party. Galpin begins moving aggressively in the outlined direction. The patrol makes good time for the next hour until in the distance they spot a band of men and a pair of dog teams, mere specks of dark moving on a sheet of white, coming in their direction. The corporal pushes ahead. The men follow. In thirty minutes the groups meet. A band of hunting Loucheaux is returning to the fort. Their dogs drag butchered caribou on a pair of sleds, the canines spread out in a fan shape each animal on its own lead.

Fraser recognizes one of the men as Njootli's cousin, one of many. He's called Kunnizzi.

"Kunnizzi, it's Constable Fraser. I see hunting's been good for your people," said the Mountie. "We're headed for the upper Caribou by tonight, then Mountain Creek Cabin tomorrow."

Kunnizzi smiles, but looks perplexed. He's quiet for awhile as he glances around him at the hills, the forest and distant mountains both to the south and behind his party in the west.

"Fraser. You make mistake. You are perhaps confused," said Kunnizzi. He, like Njootli and most of the Loucheaux, learned a fair amount of English at the hands of missionaries located in the north country. The priests roam throughout the Northwest on their driven mission to convert everyone to their beliefs, their way of thinking. They've experienced mixed results in this. Indians have become angered at times and murdered a number of the emissaries. And few of the natives take any of the teachings seriously, though a fair number of them are fascinated by the strange and unfamiliar sounds of the English language. People like the Loucheaux appear to have a natural ability to pick up different tongues and the symbols and rhythms of the priesthood prove no exception. "This way leads up high into the mountains along the divide between here and the Blackstone Valley. You can't reach the top. Far too steep. Mean cliffs. Awful drops everywhere. Only sheep walk up that way."

"We're not headed to the cabin?" asks Macdonald. "Where is it? What direction?"

"Go back way you came to the river and move along that south slope over there," said Kunnizzi as he waves a mitten-covered hand at Caribou Born Mountain. "Retrace your steps or you lose much time. Maybe even your lives. We go this way because ancestors have hunted the mountain valleys for many, many generations. You have no idea about that land. At times it is difficult for us."

The Loucheaux smiles, but his eyes betray concern and wonderment that the men are already off course so early in their run. The annual patrol is common knowledge among all the residents within a wide radius of Fort McPherson, part of this remote land's routine. And it is a chance for all of them to communicate with the outside in the form of letters.

"Are you sure of this?" asks Fraser. He looks at Galpin. The man is staring at Kinnizzi and then at the mountain. Back and forth in clear confusion.

"Very damn sure Constable," said Kunnizzi. He is vehement and a little angry in his concern and frustration. He considers all Mounties his friends, even if at times they wander about and make foolish mistakes like small children. "Turn back now. You only loose one day. Not weeks. Follow us. We'll show you the direction. Cutoff is well-known to all Loucheaux and even those crazy people up by the big water."

He's referring to the Inuits, and in particular the few that wander down this way hunting when whales and seals are scarce along the sea coast.

The party retraces its steps. The mood of the group is somber, quiet. Macdonald is aware of this and knows that he must do something.

"This happens on the trail men. Happened to me in 1909 and to Taylor two years before that," said the Inspector. "Buck up and count your blessings. Running into Kunnizzi saved us from wasted miles and days. Conserved our supplies. One day lost is no serious issue for us."

This has the desired affect. Spirits rise noticeably. Kunnizzi smiles as he recognizes that Macdonald is a leader and his worries for this patrol fade away. The men are in good hands with this one he thinks. By the time they reach the cutoff darkness holds the land. All of them, Mounties and Loucheaux alike decide to make camp. Caribou steaks, moose stew with the last of the carrots and pemmican are the main courses finished with dried apples and fruit. Raspberry tea with honey is made by Kunnizzi's brother, Natazhat. All of them eat well, then smoke their pipes. The

Loucheaux are honored with Macdonald's offering of the tinned tobacco. All of them enjoy the warmth and light of the bonfire. Snow begins to fall. Again the wolves howl, the calls seeming to emanate from all around them, and closer to camp than the other night.

"Those wolves are up to bloody work in this forest, in those hills," said Kunnizzi. The other Loucheaux nod and mutter in agreement. "When they talk in all directions at the same time there will be serious death on the land. Keep your eyes open. And hold your gun at the ready. I think that most of the game, especially the moose and the caribou that prefer these woods, have left. They have moved out into the open farther north. I don't know why. My feelings tell me this is so.

"The spirits have not been happy during our journey through this country these past weeks," said Kunnizzi. "There will be no more hunting parties of my people. The signs are not in a good order. We will stay in our lodges until things change."

On that cautionary note the men begin to turn in for the evening. Both groups have long days on the trail tomorrow, many miles to cover in their separate directions.

In the morning as the patrol runs along the southern edge of Caribou Born, beside low-rising hills that flank the mountain. The terrain is timbered and pocked with hollows that would be muskeg and shallow ponds in the summer, difficult, nearly impassable when thawed but smooth going in winter. Yesterday is largely forgotten. The men joke and urge Galpin on ahead of them as he breaks trail in the new-fallen snow. Frost hardens the trail within minutes in the increasing cold making travel easier.

As the day moves nearer sunset, dusk and then evening the dogs turn edgy, nervous. Wraith looks from side to side along the trail, his large snout tasting the air. The men begin to see wolves in the forest on all sides of them. The stealthy creatures move silently, in and out of sight, not one of them ever looking at the patrol. Their focus is on the unseen moving just beyond them. Ahead numerous tracks from moose converge in front of Galpin to form a well-packed highway littered with pellet-shaped droppings and tufts of long, dark-brown fur. The corporal has the strange feeling that men and moose are being herded by the wolves to a place of carnage. The animals have not howled or yapped once in hours. A feeling of danger, of impending violence, settles over the men, who glance constantly about them much like Wraith is doing. The corporal would like to think that this is merely a dark, slightly mad fantasy surfacing in his mind as he travels along the bleak winter trail, but the gnawing dread in his gut seems to indicate otherwise. This feeling has always been instinctual for him, a warning of trouble. His senses key up still further. Several hours after dark beneath a now clear sky jammed with stars, a half-moon and the flickering sheets of the aurora, the patrol reaches the headwaters of the Caribou River. They halt down on a flat along the streambed. The wind has packed the snow into a hard, flat surface ideal for setting up camp. It has also scoured the river ice to a hard, smooth surface that reflects the universal lights shining above.

The routine for the evening is unchanged. McConnell cooks the dried caribou they've packed, adding salt, pepper and one of the precious onions harvested from the fort's garden in the fall that are stored in a burlap sack on his sled. There's bannock, currants and tea. Throughout this time the men spot pairs of glowing eyes moving on the fringes of camp. Luminous orbs of yellow, red, and orange that flicker in and out of view as they pass behind trees. Then as the group begins to eat, the wolves are seen no more. The sled dogs are uneasy, but they dig their nests in the snow and hunker down for the night.

The four Mounties are smoking their pipes, this time

with the cheaper rag-cut tobacco, when the sound of what must be hundreds of large feet hammers down the slopes of the surrounding hills, the noise coming right at them, rumbling through the ground and up into their bodies. Tree limbs rattle and shake. The snow around the camp vibrates. Snortings, terrified bleatings accompanied by an insane chorus of high-pitched calls from the wolves rips apart the dark silence. In the moonlight the men see more than one hundred moose leap and crash onto the thick ice, hooves clattering and screeching on the slick surface, fleeing for their lives. From all directions wolves close in, eyes ablaze, jaws filled with curved, sharp teeth barred, tongues dripping saliva that reflects the fire's light. Many of them race by only feet from the Mounties. More howls, grunts, and screams pierce the air overriding the sounds of the campfire. Firelight and the waning moon's cold glow reveal a flickering, shadow-dance vision of hell. The moose have no traction on the river's surface. They slip, fall and crash into each other as they vainly attempt to flee the ravenous pack. The wolves leap, slash and slice as they hamstring the animals. They tear chunks of hide and flesh from the panicked cripples that are now far beyond terror and panic. The carnage is immense and awful to watch. Blood gouts from ripped arteries and jagged wounds in the flanks and sides of the moose. Wolves singly and in packs bring down the large creatures. Within minutes not one is standing. There are wet, bubbling sounds of last gasping breaths among the downed victims. The wolves growl and chatter among themselves in a ghastly symphony of blood lust. Sharp tearing sounds of teeth ripping still-quivering muscle from bone and tendon fill the clearing.

McConnell holds the .30-30 in a tight grip, a round levered into the chamber. The other three clutch axes. But the marauding wolves pay no heed to the men. Tonight they have only a taste for the savaged moose. Even in the flashing light of the fire – now a roaring blaze built by the men as some form of protection if only of a psychological nature – even in this primordial glow, the puddles and streams of blood stretching across the ice are can be seen clearly, the viscous liquid freezing then being covered over with another surge as the wolves rip the jugular of a barely living bull or gut a mortally injured cow who lies on her punctured belly, legs splayed at grotesque angles. The yearlings went down first and all their flesh has been devoured. Only bones and ragged pieces of hide remain of these young. The men want to turn away, but are unable to do so.

They are speechless. United in a terror that is universal and timeless. Prey and predator. The most ancient of all wilderness dances.

-CHAPTER FOUR-

There is no hunter like an Indian hunter. He will find game – if there is any around – where none but the most skillful white man will be successful.

-Major Robert F. Jones, retired
Canadian Corps of Signals

"I'VE NEVER SEEN THE LIKES OF THAT slaughter in all my years," said Galpin. "Not even on that deadly ridge in god forsaken Transvaal when that bloody Gatling gun opened up on us from above. South Africa was hell. Comrades torn to pieces on either side of me, but nothing like what those wolves visited on the hapless moose. Scraps of hide, flesh and blood everywhere. I'll not soon forget that sight."

The men are gathered around an old Marine Shipmate wood stove that is set against one rough-hewn log wall of Mountain Creek Cabin, a place of refuge well-known among all who travel this part of the remote north. The sturdy structure has saved the lives of many men desperate to escape the brutal conditions of winter over the years. The outside walls are now a rich dark brown acquired from heavy rains, thick fogs and mists. Moss is growing in the chinking and along the roof, but the cabin is still intact, secure, weather tight.

The stove was hauled up the Peel River during the summer of 1899 from the Mackenzie after being salvaged from a riverboat that wrecked on a submerged pine tree snag. The ragged trunk of the obstruction tore a hole in the wooden hull sending the *Hazel B No. 4* to an early retirement, the hard-working vessel foundered on a muddy bank many stream miles above the Arctic Circle. A pair of gold prospectors bound for the upper reaches of the Peel persuaded the pilot of the *Sikanni Chief* to hold near shore while they searched for salvageable goods that turned out to include the Shipmate that was only lightly rusted from its stay on the mud flat. They also turned up a barrel of rum that somehow had been overlooked during the abandonment. A small treasure that loomed large in the hearts and minds of the two adventurers for many days and nights. The men pulled, winched and man-handled the stove onto a small raft constructed from scavenged planks, beams and rope found on the *Hazel B.* and then they loaded it onboard the larger craft. They dismantled the stove in pieces as small as possible, though several weighed more than one hundred pounds each. They stored these beneath a canvas tarp back from the water along the riverbank. Over the course of three months they took turns making the run from the mouth of the Peel River on the Mackenzie to where the Wind River joins the Peel at their construction site, a journey of more than one hundred and fifty river miles. And then one of them would head back downriver again for another load. The gold seekers had alternated between one of them building the weather-tight, sturdy cabin that Macdonald and his men find themselves in on this blustery winter's night plus working a nearby claim, and the other one running the wild river living on grayling, Dolly Vardon and any game he might shoot along the way. They would make the trip as fast as possible running for as many as eighteen hours a day in the perpetual daylight of the warm months. When the pair had finished their endeavors the main room was twenty-by-eighteen feet with a low loft that was a little more than half this size. The cabin was warm courtesy of the stove and the excellent construction and attention to weather proofing the prospectors had given the cabin. The pair worked the claim on the small creek that tumbled out of the surrounding mountains for five years. They never became fabulously rich, but when they returned for the outside world, they each had bank accounts of nearly $12,000 – far better than most in the Yukon in those heady, tempestuous gold rush years that saw dreams shattered, fortunes made and squandered, and men murdered over worthless claims.

The temperature has fallen thirty degrees in the past two days to minus fifty-four Fahrenheit and the wind is driving the snow down and along the ground at a fearful pace, the howling eerily reminiscent of the massacre of three nights ago. Hard weather conditions and the somber spirits of the men turn the two-day run from the upper Caribou River into a three-day grind that takes on nightmarish proportions as an enormous cold front washes over the men bringing with it the heaviest snows and strongest winds of the season. Their surroundings at midday are dim, surreally twilight in nature. Even Wraith Dhogge is affected by the gloom as the hound acts subdued though pulling more than his share. When they reach the cabin Macdonald tells the men that they will layover for a day to regroup, fix any gear that is damaged and to look for game in the area. Moose are normally abundant here either working upstream from the Bonnet Plume River's junction with the Peel or in the hills to the west. Caribou are often sighted in the valley, too.

"Nor will I ever forget any of it, either," said Fraser. "And the coppery, almost sweet smell of all of that blood. I can't seem to get that out of my nose or maybe it's embedded in my memory, like the dying screams of all of those moose. Horrible. Plain horrible."

"Kunnizzi warned us that this would happen, that there would be death on the land," said McConnell. "Though what we could have done differently I'll never know. The wolves kept pace with us for miles almost as though they wanted us to see the massacre. I felt like I was being herded along like the moose. Sometimes fate seals a man's life up tightly in its own strange web and all he can hope for is to survive and to move on from there."

They puff on their pipes and shift in their chairs.

"I agree," said Galpin. He put two more pieces of wood in the stove that had warmed the cabin to sixty degrees. The door to the firebox was left open providing an orange glow to the surroundings. Macdonald was busy updating his journals by the light of two candles wedged into rum bottles he found on one of the shelves. He drank his measure of whiskey from a tin cup and drew on his pipe while he worked at this duty. The other men sit on rough chairs made of birch with seats of woven bark. They are gathered around the stove working on their pipes and taking small sips of the Scotch. "I don't believe in omens when it comes to completing one's duty such as this patrol, but something as gruesome, as ghastly as what those wolves did makes one think bad thoughts. It's hard for me not to imagine of foul fates waiting for us on the trail even though I know better."

They all nod as if they've been thinking the same thought.

"One summer back home a band of male Red Stag had moved up to the heather meadows along a string of tarns that ran beneath rock cliffs a few miles from my village," said Fraser. "Magnificent animals with wide racks fully formed by late August. As large as those of the caribou. Early, before dawn , or sometimes at dusk I'd stalk them. Not hunting to kill them for meat or a trophy, but to get close to them, to observe their behavior. I'd bring my father's binoculars and crawl the last hundred yards along the ground to a stone outcropping that looked down on the water where they preferred to drink. There were dozens of males. No does. They still remained separate until the fall rut, isolated from the bucks and holding lower down in our country.

"Late one night, a full moon it was, the wolves set up a tremendous, unearthly noise, calling in a way that brought home the meaning of 'blood curdling,'" said Fraser. "All of the dogs in the village barked in accompaniment for hours. They sounded frightened. No, more as though they were terrified. The din continued on for hours and I imagined that I could hear screams from other animals up by those cliffs. In the morning I went to my vantage point and looked through the glasses. Such a sight I'd never seen before and not again until the other night. Fur, chunks of torn skin, savaged heads exposing bloody skulls with the racks still attached to them, blood all over the ground cover and staining the deep blue of the little lakes copper brown. God, it was awful, beyond anything horrible I'd ever considered. Since that day, I've always carried a pistol or rifle when walking in that country. The wolves will kill anything. They've proven that to me. Humans are prey to them, too."

They share other tales and myths regarding the species.

Macdonald lets the men go on this way, sensing that they are exorcising the event from their lives, or at least putting it into manageable proportions. This is healthy and a necessary process he reasons and continues his writing.

"One evening after I'd first been posted to McPherson I was on the bank watching the river after dinner when Njootli came up," said McConnell. "We didn't know each other very well yet, as if anyone ever really figures out that crazy Loucheaux to begin with. He lit his own pipe. It was filled with awful smelling stuff. Reminded me of the stockyards in Edmonton. Simply terrible, but he seemed to enjoy it. No accounting for personal preference sometimes."

"Please advance your story," said Macdonald from his corner seat at the small table. "We must make Dawson City before spring thaw, you understand."

The men, including McConnell, laugh, the first time since the slaughter at Caribou River.

"Well, we talked of this and that – trapping, netting char in the Peel, the differences between polar bears and grizzlies, and about timber wolves," said the constable. "Then he was quiet for a bit before turning to me and saying, 'You know constable, those wolves are god-damnit-to-hell smart. One cold winter as I camped on the other side of the mountains long miles south of here along the Blackstone, I watched as more of those demons than I can count drove many moose onto the frozen river and killed them all. They raced in and out of those moose snarling, biting and murdering. Nothing left in the morning but bloody ice and chewed up fur. You bet I made it as fast as these legs would move through the snow to my cousin's village. I never want to see that vision again. Not ever in these eyes. Not a healthy sight for a man. Those wolves are owners of this land. Never forget this.' And then he turned away from the river and me, and walked back to his hut. He is a strange one often enough, but Njootli knows this land and how it operates better than any of us. I listen to him, always."

The constable pauses and stares into the fire before continuing.

"I'd forgotten the story until just now," said McConnell. "This country is a hard place and we will do well to respect its power and our own insignificance. I plan on staying as humble as this body is capable of until we reach Dawson. Then I may let loose some, but not until that time when we are safely among others in a place filled with warmth and light. Then I'll grin, laugh and flirt with the ladies of the town."

"R.G., did you notice that since that night we've not seen any game. No moose, caribou, even porcupine and those spiky devils are usually all over the place?" asks Fraser. "No fresh tracks in the snow, either. It's like what the wolves did has driven all of the animals away from the river, like they've all fled this country. Maybe Kunnizzi was right about the game having moved out of the area. I hope he's wrong."

"I haven't spotted any fresh tracks or sign in the three days since and that's nearly fifty miles of trail," said Galpin. "It's unusual and makes me uneasy. We'll need more meat. Not just for ourselves but for our dogs. They've put in long, hard days and have been wonderful in the traces. That Wraith is a leader. I noticed two of the dogs were slacking yesterday. He only had to turn that big head of his and look at the pair. Next I noticed they were pulling harder than any of them. Talk about a leader. But they eat a frightening amount of fish. We need them strong and alert to be successful in our assignment. That requires meat. Lots of it."

Macdonald finishes his diary and signs the day's entry as is his custom. He reloads and lights his pipe.

"Corporal, I appreciate your concern, but this country is thick with animals even in the most desolate of weather," said the Inspector. "We'll do fine, but I think we'll hedge our bets when we leave day after tomorrow. You've had the last two days on the sleds. And tomorrow is something of a day of rest. You're our strongest man in the lead. I want you to head out an hour before we follow in the sleds. Make that 6:30. You'll have a chance to spot game well away from the clatter we make on the trail. And constables, I want both of you out looking for game by eight tomorrow morning. The more meat we can obtain now, the better we'll all look at the remainder of the journey. Understood?"

"Yes, sir." The three said in unison.

"Sound ideas. And in the morning I'll re-stitch some of the harness and gather more wood. May as well be warm while we can." said Galpin. Macdonald nods and adds that he'll be doing much the same.

"Tomorrow being New Year's Eve, I think that we'll have an extra ration of this fine Scotch whiskey," said Macdonald as he savors another sip. "From the following day on out it will be a straight push to Dawson, but a night's ease around our warm friend here," and he points to the old stove, "will welcome the new year in grand style and do wonders for our stamina."

The men nod, smile and turn their conversation to the mundane details of their travels today. Macdonald has his land-born ship and its crew back sailing on an even keel.

"If you like, let me show you our course for the next week," said Galpin a little later in the evening. He retrieves a tube containing the maps, pulls them out and unrolls the appropriate one. He spreads this out before Macdonald on the small table that has the initials E.M. and S.H. along with 1901 carved into it. Perhaps they are those of the prospectors and the year they struck color.

"We'll be running up the Wind River along the west bank and passing beneath Mount Deception and Mount Deslauriers will be off to the east some miles but still visible," said Galpin. "Then we'll edge through the canyon that cuts through the Illtyd Range where we strike up westward along the Little Wind until we reach the fork that gives way to Forrest Creek. We must pass through the Illtyd gap on the ice, but the cold should ensure that there is no overflow to freeze our feet or those of the dogs'."

"Hard ice with no slush on it and powdery snow is what I wish our venture" said Macdonald. "How many miles to the pass in the mountains, corporal?"

"I make ninety-five, perhaps one hundred," said Galpin. "Six days, seven at most."

"Very good," said Macdonald. "Make sure the rifle is in good shape for the morning. Then let's all turn in. Tomorrow's the last day of 1910. Let's make it a productive one."

The next day finds Fraser and McConnell working their way up the south fork of Mountain Creek for hours without success, without even the faintest suggestion of success. They'd hoped to bring down a moose, quarter it and return to the cabin to hitch up the dogs and haul back the meat. Even a small caribou would have been welcome. No such luck. They've seen no sign of life since they left Macdonald and Galpin to their chores this morning. The sliding indentations of their snowshoes are the only marks in the six inches of new snow that fell last night. There haven't been any signs of game, no caribou, moose or rabbit tracks or droppings. No ravens squawking overhead. Not even the call of a wolf. There are not any chickadees hopping from branch to branch in the dense canopy of dry limbs that crowd out the sky. The land is lifeless. The wind is down. It has been so since daybreak. The mountain peaks are invisible in the low cloud cover that is a uniform gray that appears motionless. The summits may not exist anymore, perhaps washed away by the omnipresent gloom. The sun's light is filtered to the extent that the trees don't cast shadows. Everything is a field of white that merges imperceptibly with the gray above. Small flakes of snow slowly drift down from the clouds. The entire landscape, the bleak winter setting, is featureless, without dimension. From another world. The only way the men can tell where they are is by keeping next to the banks on either side of the frozen stream or working up the icy surface. When they stray from the streambed either the rough sides of the wash or the thick tree line force them back on course.

Checking his silver pocket watch, Fraser sees that it is past noon. They stop and eat some pemmican, a handful or two of dried currents. They take swigs of cold tea that has been kept from freezing in a leather sack kept close to Fraser's body. The food and drink are without flavor, featureless like the land. They do this without speaking.

There is nothing to say. No words can add to or expand on the morning's futility. The men's senses have been worn numb by the relentless sameness of this natural nothingness. The two of them look up the creek drainage and behind them into the mountains. Directly across from them the spruce trees are buried in snow. White. All white. Nothing but whiteness. Soundless. Unchanging. Disorienting. It is like being trapped in a chamber with no dimension or form. Even the lower surfaces of the clouds are this timeless white as they take on, absorb, reflect the only color that appears left in the world. The trunks and limbs of the trees, the pine needles are all white in a thick coating of hoar frost that descended upon the forest in the night. The buffs, browns, and blacks of their parkas and fur hats are sprinkled with snow. The garments no longer offer faint visual relief in a landscape turned featureless, growing invisible as time imperceptibly passes. Even the Mounties' clothing is now covered in frost, their body heat not penetrating to the exterior, a layer of the blanketing ice crystals has spread over the leather and fur, over their beards. The men are blending into, becoming a part of the frozen land. Only the light of life glowing in their eyes provides any relief from the monotone vision.

There is nothing to see, to attract one's attention as they stand motionless in the white. No sound. Only the slight movement of their icy breath rising thinly through wool scarves covering their mouths and noses. The slight moisture dissipates inches above their heads. The falling of the few random snow flakes has stopped.

Without speaking they agree to turn and retrace their steps back down the creek bed to the cabin – its warmth, shelter and illusion of life are an outpost in this frozen desolation. They push through the snow, their webbed foot gear sinking down into the softness several inches with each step. By the time they spot the glow of candle and fire light coming from the structure's windows darkness has taken over the land. Impenetrable. No star light. No moon shimmer. No aurora radiance. The mantel of clouds blocks all of this. The country is closed in on them Shut down. They are physically and mentally exhausted, drained of all energy. Other then their two comrades inside the cabin, their isolation from other men is complete.

They move to the door. Wraith hears their approach and barks in greeting though even his deep-throated voice dies quickly on the still air. The other dogs set up a tremendous racket, barking, pawing the ground, rattling their chains. The men are heartened by the chaos, the familiarity of a place they've known little more than a day. From within they hear the sounds of talking and laughter, of life. They remove their snowshoes and stack them against the wall. The door creaks on heavy iron hinges as they shove its weight inward. A blast of warmth greets them, melting the frost from their scarves and their beards. They've returned. This is sanctuary in the middle of all of this whiteout nothingness.

Macdonald looks up and immediately senses the two men's mood.

"Welcome, men," he said. "The corporal is preparing our dinner. A hearty stew of gourmandish dimensions – moose, caribou, potatoes, carrots, onions. It's New Year's Eve. There will be mounds of apples and currants, and the bannock."

"We sighted no game the entire time, Sir. Not even any tracks. There's nothing out there at all," said McConnell. Fraser removes his out mittens, then the wool liners. He pulls his parka over his head and shakes off the moisture. The other man does the same. "The land is empty. It feels like we're walking through a gigantic ghost ship. Like we're the only ones left alive in all the world."

"Cheer up, constable," said the Inspector. "The

northern lands are like that sometimes. No game to be found. Dead silence. Cold. Nothing but white. Can play fearsome games on a man's mind if he indulges himself. Tonight our cabin here is warm. We have food and we have drink. Most importantly we have each other. We'll not only survive, we'll flourish. Come to the fire lads. There's no limit on the grog this night. Here drink up. Let's celebrate the night as men of destiny in a great country with a grand mission to be completed."

And they accept mugs of the whiskey as Macdonald claps both of them on the back with firm hands. If the emptiness and winter desolation concerns this man, he's showing no sign of it. Quite the contrary.

"The corporal and I have gone over the maps. Our course is clear. All of our gear is in full readiness. The dogs are fed and rested," he said, and sips from his mug, drops of whiskey clinging to his mustache. "We'll surely bring down some animals on our way up the Wind and Little Wind or in the narrow canyon of Forrest Creek leading through the mountains. Even if we don't succeed here, we've calculated that there is more than enough fish for the dogs and provisions for ourselves until we drop down into the Blackstone where the caribou are gathered up by the thousands, not to mention all of the moose. More meat is always welcome, but we're in good shape. We may have to ration to some extent, but we'll survive. We will keep a tight rein on the disbursement of the fish and the meat. You two pursued your task with determination today. That's all any man can ask."

Both men are silent, but their expressions lighten at the inspector's compliment.

"Yee gods men. We could be trapped in the filthy air of Glasgow choking on all of that sooty coal smoke or be confined in cramped quarters on some destitute steamer tramping the Atlantic," said Macdonald. "We're alive in a great land. Drink up. Cheers to all of us. Tomorrow the adventure of our assignment awaits us. A full life with purpose. We are blessed, indeed."

Now they drink deeply. Fraser and McConnell's faces are bright red from the transition from cold to warmth coupled with the buoyant, infectious mood of their leader and the burn of the whiskey in their stomachs. Life seems real to them again. They are no longer in a zone between one lifeless world and another of even more frightening possibilities that they can only sense, can vaguely glimpse from the corners of their eyes. Warmth. The smell of food, the whiskey, the promise of a night spent with good companions, all of this has rejuvenated their spirits.

Galpin ladles the steaming stew into bowls. In the middle of the small table a plate is piled with the fruit. Pieces of the hard bread, broken into pieces, are stacked on another plate. He pours tea into their mugs. Macdonald adds a modest measure of whiskey to each. The fire is stoked. The candles light the setting with a comfortable brightness that flickers and casts animated shadows of the men's actions along the timbered walls.

The men rise early on this first day of 1911. They are in good spirits. It's six a.m. and still several hours to sunrise of around ten. Living in the Arctic takes some getting used to and requires an adaptable temperament. Summertime sees sunlight all day and the winter offers at the most this far north five hours of daylight. Many individuals find the extremes and the rapid fluctuations between them to be too much to bear. Adjusting to the abnormal, at least by the standards of the lower latitudes, is a shock to most internal time clocks. The four Mounties are well-used to the abnormality and pay it little attention. Though they each consumed a fair amount of whiskey the night before, none of them show any signs of over-indulgence, of hangovers. They are fit, tough, resilient, and not given to extended bouts of drinking. One night on an average of every couple of months at the most suits these men fine. More than whiskey is needed to slow them down.

The night of revelry has done much to put the events of the past few days behind them. The dogs pull with eagerness and energy lunging against the leather of their traces. Wraith is in fine form, pounding along the trail that the Corporal had made earlier this morning. That day sees them make good time. They camp about halfway from the junction of the Wind and Peel rivers. An Inuit inukshuk, a pile of rocks resembling a man, marks an old hunting trail or perhaps the way to a fertile valley filled with game in milder times. The marker is set on a hill near camp. Galpin did not spot any game, though he crossed the trail of what he guessed to be a band of perhaps fifteen caribou. The sign in the form of pellet-shaped scat the size of marbles was several days old, but encouraging none the less. At least animals were working through the country the men were moving into.

The next day breaks clear and cold, minus fifty. The sky is pure deep blue and the sun shines brightly even though it clings to the horizon far in the south, just managing to rise fully above the mountain peaks for a few minutes. Galpin continues in his role as the trail blazer. Within a few miles of starting out he comes upon a pair of porcupines gnawing on a piece of wood that looks to be a plank washed downstream in last spring's flood. Perhaps it's part of an abandoned gold mine sluice box. He fires twice, hitting his mark both times. He then carefully skins out the animals avoiding the stinging bite of the sharp quills as he does so. He wraps the meat in burlap he carries for the purpose and waits for the others.

He sips tea and chews a hunk of pemmican. He looks at his surroundings and marvels at the austere beauty and magnificence of the Arctic north. The land is untouched and he imagines that it has looked much like this a thousand years ago, maybe ten thousand years past.

Across the river and far up on the slopes Galpin thinks he spots several specks, off-white in color, moving along the scoured face of an avalanche chute. Could his eyes be playing tricks on him? Is his mind merely fabricating the objects and their movement after so many hours of scanning for life in this barren landscape? He marks the location on the slope in his mind and then digs out his Zeiss binoculars. A friend bought these for him on a trip to Germany over ten years ago and shortly after the manufacturer had gone into large commercial production in 1894. They are a spectacular instrument with impeccable optics. An invaluable tool for him in the wilds. He sights in on the place where he thought he saw the animals. He works the lenses of the glasses back and forth, up and down along the mountain, but fails to find any animals, the sheep or goats he thought of initially. He tightens the focus and notices a line crossing the chute that looks like a fresh disturbance in the snow that is otherwise smooth, pristine, for as far as he can see in all directions. He stares through the lenses with intense concentration. His eyes begin to water. He wipes them on the furred cuff of his parka and looks again. Maybe the disturbance is that of animal tracks, maybe it's only a flickering distortion that is the function of both distance and the angle of the sun. He gives up in frustration. What difference would it have made if he had actually spotted a band of sheep? They would be miles away and working across a slope that would be impossible to reach let alone climb. Well, at least he would have seen some bigger animals. A slight reassurance in the midst of all of this lifelessness. He laughs aloud at his small desperation here and pushes the incident from his mind.

Galpin hears the dogs well before he sees them pulling the sleds as they emerge from the trees several hundred yards distant. The sun reflects off of the men's goggles that are working well in preventing the excruciating pain of snow blindness. Fortunately the dogs rarely succumb to the problem. When they pull up even with him, he packs the dressed meat away beneath the tarp and on top of the dried moose and caribou. The scent of fresh blood makes the dogs nervous, edgy. They've not fully recovered from the moose slaughter.

"It's not much, but it's an evening's stew," said Galpin. "I for one am grateful."

"Your efforts are appreciated," said Macdonald. "Any meat for the pot is welcome. Porcupine will offer us a change of fare. A touch of variety. And we, too, are grateful both for this provender and for your steady efforts."

"I'll push on and wait for you as soon as I find a flat location to set up camp," said the corporal. "I think we can make it some distance past the southern edge of Mount Deception. This snow tracks well and the dogs look fit. Is this acceptable to you, Inspector?"

"Lead on and we shall follow with vigor," said Macdonald. His dry humor constantly defuses any stress that was building among his men. "Sally forth my good man."

Galpin laughs as do Fraser and McConnell while shaking their heads. They may be totally isolated in the hard heart of the wilderness, but the patrol is confident in the eventuality of a positive outcome to this journey. They are in good shape and are making excellent time. The day has warmed to minus twenty-five. Warm enough to take the bitter edge out of the air, but not so warm as to turn the snow sticky and a hindrance to travel. Conditions should remain excellent for the remainder of the day.

With that Galpin steps lively through the snow, his progress marked by a whooshing sound as he sinks in the powder and then raises his feet to move forward. The others drink some cold tea poured from a leather flask and munch pieces of brittle bannock as they rest and allow him to forge ahead so that he might have at least a fighting chance of jumping any game that may be in the area. Dogs being dogs, they never travel anywhere without announcing their presence with heavy breathing, barks, yips, yowls and assorted mewlings, not to mention the strong scent they cast.

Several hours after dark, sunset coming along in mid-afternoon, the men spot the orange flickers and myriad sparks of a fire. Within a quarter of an hour they pull up to a wide bench above the river that is both open and also sheltered by a tall stand of pine and birch that breaks the force of wind that streams down from the mountains that hem in the Wind River along the northwestern side of the drainage. The river has formed a broad path here leaving piles of rock and gravel in braids that divide the current into a number of narrow channels that are clearly seen in the starlight and glow of the northern lights even with all of the snow on the ground and ice. The rocky islands rise as much as six feet above the frozen river. Dark shapes of sharp-peaked mountains tower above them in the east. Mount Deception rises directly above camp like an enormous jet-black sentinel that guards the way into the high country accessed by the Little Wind River and Forrest Creek. Mount Deslauriers is a dark form in the distance. The lesser but no less severe summits of the Illtyd Range block the southern horizon some miles distant like a well-laid stone wall. The Wind River must have gnawed away at this rock for many thousands of years to carve the gap through the mountains that the patrol will pass through tomorrow. The relentless liquid mix of rock turned to fine powder by the pressure of glaciers and ice fields far back and above the valley, along with sand and rock, continually grinds down and through the ancient stone of the mountains as century after century passes. In so many ways measurements of time mean absolutely nothing in a land marked by near-eternal patience.

Galpin has already built a roaring blaze, gathered a mound of wood nearly as tall as he is, cleared spots for the tents and covered them in spruce bows. He's also cut and trimmed a brace of logs for the Yukon stove. A stack of wood, uniform in length, is next to the cooking area. Macdonald sees all of this completed work and smiles.

"Damn good man," he thinks. "Give me a dozen more like him and like these other two and I'll tame this country and make this a fit place for anyone to live in. These men make me proud to be a part of the Service. There are none better anywhere."

He guides his team to a spot on the edge of the campsite where he releases and stakes the dogs one at a time. He then feeds them before attending to his own gear and the communal equipment and food of the men. The dogs' needs come first. There welfare is vital and they cannot completely care for themselves.

"I shot another porcupine. They seem to have taken over the forest. Possibly their fierce nature is responsible for driving away the larger animals," said Galpin. He is laughing, but he also wonders where all of the moose and caribou have gone. "Maybe we'll live on them while the dogs eat fish and our dried moose. Whatever it takes, we'll make our way to Dawson, eh men."

The rest of them agree. In this country at this time of the year food is food, no matter what manner of creature it comes from. And the meat from porcupine at this time of year is excellent. They enjoy the stew McConnell prepares along with the ubiquitous bannock and currants. He's become the outfit's cook by silent agreement among all four of them. The fact that he's stashed delights such as onions and some spices sealed his culinary fate for the trip. And

McConnell clearly enjoys the work, often whistling and talking to himself about preparation details, flavorings and the taste of the food as though there is a group of cooks seeing to the men's meals, instead of this one cheerful man.

After the enjoyable nightly ritual of smoking pipes while standing around the fire, the men turn in. The soft comfort and warmth of their eiderdown bags a welcome escape from the day's rigors along the trail. Soon the sounds of snoring from the exhausted men resound about the campsite. Macdonald lays four large pieces of wood on the pile of glowing coals that shimmer in waves of intense heat that fluctuate between crimson and hot orange looking like miniature cities lit up for the night. The inspector notes in his log entry for today, January 2nd, that they've made twenty-two miles. He's pleased. At this rate, by tomorrow they'll reach the fork of the Little Wind. Within five or six days after that with a steady pace and reasonable weather they should cross over the Wernecke Mountains at Hart Divide. From there he believes that it will be all an easy course downhill to their final destination, a smooth glide to Dawson City and civilization. He's a bit tired as he's noticed the others are, but that's to be expected. They've pushed along steadily in difficult conditions. And the run to Dawson City has never been considered an easy go of it to begin with. Macdonald feels that all is going as it should be, according to plan and that they are on schedule. He watches the fire from the comfort of his bag and enjoys the fierce silence of this wild place.

The patrol makes steady progress all the next morning and into the afternoon. A couple of inches of dry snow fell overnight providing a smooth, slick surface for the sleds' runners to glide over. The sky is clear again and a timeless blue that casts a hint of its color over the otherwise totally white land. The sun's radiance has pushed the temperature up to a relatively warm minus-fifteen degrees. Where the

Wind River exits the canyon through a narrow gap along the northern slope of the Illtyd Mountains the men are forced to drop down to the river. There is no way along the edge, only precipitous rock walls. Climbing up and over the mountains to reach the river on the upstream side would take days and most likely be impossible at this time of the year. They must line each sled down the twenty-foot banks that abut the river using lengths of rope held by the four of them so that the weight does not overtake and crush the dogs. They wrap the ropes around a large spruce trunk to gain even more leverage. Friction rubs the bark off the tree and leaves a clean band of tan wood four feet up the base. The lining is completed without incident, but the men are actually perspiring some and they are huffing as they regain their breath. Fraser relieves Galpin of the trail breaking duty. The corporal takes over working the third sled.

All of them probe the snow regularly with poles cut and shaped from willows along the banks. They're doing all they can to avoid slushy areas of river overflow. With the warming temperatures and the direct sunlight this could become a problem. A drenching of any of their feet will require an immediate halt, the building of a large fire and quick drying of feet and clothes if severe frostbite is to be avoided. So far their vigilance has prevented this calamity. They've been fortunate and are hopeful that they will continue to have this luck.

The rays of the sun flash intensely through a notch in the Wernecke Mountains rising in the south. The tops of the Illtyds are lost from view far above the party, blocked out by sheer walls of limestone that once was the floor of a vast inland sea. The cliffs rise well over a thousand feet above them, the rock shining in deep shades of ochre, tan and gray. Dissolved mineral deposits stain the walls in streaks of green, orange and rust. Bands of white, green and reddish quartz streak the rock walls. The color is a welcome relief from all of the monotony of the white snow. The day has been without wind or even a breeze, but as they approach the chasm entrance a cold blast shoots through the opening and on it is the taste of hard ice and snow. The dogs involuntarily shiver and the men pull their fur hoods closer about their heads. The way through the mountains by this narrow crease is several miles long. The Wind River climbs quickly through what must be fierce, impassable cascades, whirlpools and rapids in spring and summer. The rock cliffs pinch in ever closer as the patrol works its way upriver navigating around enormous boulders lodged in the stream corridor. Lighter-colored sections in the mountains indicate where the obstructions have been sheered off by the action of ice, frost and erosion to crash down into the Wind.

Falling rock pitches off the sides of the canyon, bouncing far out into space before slamming into the snow or bouncing off the iron-hard river ice. One of these projectiles hitting a man in the head would mean death. They keep a sharp eye out in what they realize is a largely futile attempt to avoid being injured.

Looking up the men watch as a string of seven Dall sheep make their way across a ledge that is invisible from the distance of hundreds of feet below standing on the frozen Wind. The first big game they've spotted in days and many miles. The animals' horns are impressive, enormous curls the color of flat bronze that sweep in complete circles on both sides of their regal heads. The thick fur of the animals is another shade of white, a more subdued hue than the snow that covers the land in a carpet many feet thick. The sound of the sheep's hooves clattering across the exposed stone is muted by the distance of the elevation. The leader pauses and looks down on the unnatural assemblage below him. Men, dogs, sleds, objects he has probably never seen. Satisfied that none of this is a threat, he resumes moving along the sheer face of the cliff. In seconds they vanish from view, the spectral forms lost behind a serrated outcropping that leans out over the river.

"I'd have liked to have taken a shot at those," said Fraser. "Maybe if I'd hit one it would have fallen into our laps. Then we'd be dining on roast mutton tonight. By the time I had one of them in my sights, he disappeared behind those rocks. Then they were all gone."

"Game moves fast in this country, eh," said Macdonald.

They continue up river.

The sun drops behind the far peaks and deep purple shadows cover the canyon, engulfing both men and dogs in a frigid murkiness. The wind is now roaring, creating a piercing screeching sound as the air is compressed and forces its way through the narrow limestone passage much like the flood waters of spring runoff will do six months from now. The air spins and washes in roiling waves of ice crystals as it shoots through the opening. Progress is slow for the patrol. Time passes. The stars and aurora begin to shine. The North Star radiates like a beacon over their shoulders. The group is still over a mile from the open, flat valley that they can see through the canyon, level benches leading up to the forest showing a rich blue in the evening's sky light.

Suddenly the gales stops. It's gone. Completely, like the raging force was never here in the first place. The land is silent. The actions of men urging dogs, and those dogs straining and barking, echo hollowly off of the cliffs that climb up above the icy surface of the river. The noise ricochets back and forth among the walls in parody of the original sounds. The crisp papery shushing of runners slipping over the snow is brittle, unnatural in this place that seems more tomb than river corridor.

Eventually the patrol nears the end of this stark passage through the Illtyds, the quiet mountains seeming to look down and observe the progress of the patrol as it makes its way to the south. Perhaps these shapes pass their own geologic judgment on the actions of beings that are attempting to defy the winter threat posed by the Arctic. Or, as is more likely, the mountains are only mountains that impede the progress of Macdonald and his men. Mountains that are not alive, they have no emotion whatsoever. The Wind River opens before them no more than one hundred yards away, its course slanting southeastward into a place of uncharted mountains and valleys. They will continue up the Little Wind beginning tomorrow. Above the canyon at the confluence this river is as wide and deep as the Wind. The Little Wind runs due south for a dozen miles before angling southwest to its junction with Forrest Creek. Macdonald spots an ideal location to pitch camp on the near or western bank perhaps no more than a quarter-mile away. They are all tired from the long day and the inhospitable, foreboding canyon. A fire, food, and sleep are what's needed now. The silence of this place is eerie, even to an experienced man like the Inspector. The quiet is unnatural in his mind.

In an instant a distant roaring from far above the river reaches their ears. The rumbling grows to that of a thousand steam engines pounding down on the men. An avalanche has let loose from an invisible mountain face near the summit line. The sound of its incredible energy and motion hums and reverberates through the narrow space sliced between all of the rock.

"Go hard, men," said Macdonald as he whips his team into action. "Run for it. The whole damned mountain is coming down on us."

All of them push for all they're worth, for their lives. The dogs sense imminent death and pull like they never have before in their lives. Men, dogs, sleds race towards the opening and safety. The distance narrows as the thundering of the slide builds in intensity as it races down on the group. A wind generated at the head of all of the crashing material, blows over the patrol, whips them along to even greater effort. Miniature devil winds kick up the snow on the river's surface ahead of them, the small tornados spinning and whirling like insane tops that bounce into each other and then carom away to opposite sides of the ice like boxers being separated by a referee. The patrol clears the cliffs and continues moving as hard as it can. Each man turns and looks behind him. A wall of snow and rock shoots out over the canyon and plummets hundreds of feet towards the frozen river. Boulders the size of log cabins slam into the far wall exploding into pieces larger than the sleds and crash down and through the ice. Water shoots up through the holes and freezes instantly, falling back in a frozen mist. Entire trees soar into space like gigantic spears. Some of them smash and shatter into mangled chunks against the limestone. Shards of rock rain down on the Mounties. Chunks of stone and ice whistle past them, slamming into the white spruce trees and the earthen banks far ahead. A jagged missile hits the lead dog of McConnell's sled crushing its head instantly. Smaller pieces pelt the men and dogs. Snow billows out of the canyon and envelopes the patrol in a choking cloud. All light is gone. They are in a maelstrom of pitch darkness that is part whirlwind, part gale that knocks the men down, rolls the sleds into the terrified dogs and then rushes upriver dissipating as it reaches a far bend.

Everything is covered in snow. A couple of feet of the stuff. The men stand and check to see if they have broken bones or lacerations, to see if they are still alive. None of them have been injured seriously. Bruises and small cuts are the worst of it. The most serious casualty is the death of the lead dog and a piece of rock stuck in the flank of another that cries in pain and terror. Finding a replacement that works as hard as the dead leader will be difficult. Dogs are not often interchangeable parts in a sled team. The men will have to make do with the animals that remain.

"Lord god almighty, what in the hell happened?" said Fraser. "I thought we were finished."

"An avalanche of a size that I've never witnessed," said Macdonald. "The sun's heat this afternoon loosened the snow on the high slopes above us and then the quick cooling of night set the mess loose on us. Is everyone okay?"

They all report in the affirmative and spend the next hour righting the sleds, repacking gear and provisions and removing the dead and the injured dogs from their traces. The other canines sniff in the direction of their two mates when the men carry them back to the last sled where the dead one is wrapped in a piece of canvas and the other, its wound now bandaged, is secured to the top of the load wrapped in a wool blanket.

"We've been lucky here, men," said Macdonald. "I know you may find this hard to believe, but I consider what just occurred to be an omen, a sign of the good fortune that seems to be following us on our journey. Think on it when you've the time. Those wolves of last week did not descend on us. No, they attacked the moose. And this avalanche, which surely could have buried us alive or crushed the life from all of us, fell after, admittedly just after, we'd cleared the canyon. Luck is with us alright. Lets head to that bank up there and make camp."

Galpin takes another look behind him. Eighty, ninety feet of snow, ice and rock blocks the river's entrance to the grave they've narrowly escaped. Rocks and chunks of ice continue to slide over the cliff's edge. Rivulets of snow resembling frozen springs pour down onto the debris.

"If this is luck," he said as he surveys the mound of wreckage blocking the canyon's entrance, "then I pray I never see real misfortune on this trip."

139

The men and even the dogs are quiet at camp as they settle into their nightly routine. The heat and light of a huge fire help to lighten the mood some as does a spicy moose stew with the last of the carrots and potatoes. The dogs eat their ration of dried fish in near silence. There is none of the usual growling and bickering that normally accompanies the feeding frenzy. Even the malamutes that are normally combative among each other dutifully consume their food then scratch out their beds in the hard snow, curl up and go to sleep.

Small slides of ice and rock continue into the night with bangs, whooshes and cracks of tree trunks and limbs rolling over the cliff and smashing far below on the accumulated rubble from the avalanche. Clouds move in swiftly blotting out the stars and intense aurora.

The injured dog dies shortly after the others fall asleep.

Macdonald passes around the imported pipe tobacco. The men smoke in silence while standing close to the fire. The temperature is now at minus-thirty-five and falling gradually .

"Sir, I realize that we'll have no problems passing through the Wernecke's and Hart Pass, ultimately reaching our destination, but I think that it would be prudent if we butchered the two dogs and cached the meat here in the unlikely event that we were forced to come down off those mountains and make a retreat back to McPherson," said Galpin. "This may seem an unnecessary and barbaric measure at this point, but we've always done the prudent thing on our expeditions and I feel that this action with regards to the dogs would be another."

No one speaks. McConnell throws more wood on the blaze. Fraser turns his back on the flames to warm it. Macdonald puffs away on his pipe, the smoke blowing into his face from the breeze that now carries scattered snow flakes. A wolf howls from somewhere on the slopes above the canyon.

"What you say has merit," said the inspector. "You and Fraser see to it now before the meat is frozen as hard as Sheffield steel. And do the chore over there on the edge of the bank and away from the other dogs. No use sending the fear of death through them if we can avoid doing so,"

Fraser is not eager to skin the dogs, animals that completed loyal and hard duty for the men only a few hours before, but he understands the wisdom of Galpin's suggestion and Macdonald's order. He agrees with it. They drag the bundled dog carcasses from camp and proceed with their grisly job. Skinning the dogs, both of them mixed breeds and not malamutes, takes time in the cold. The meat is nearly frozen but their razor-sharp knife blades make the cutting go smoothly and quickly. They package the fifty pounds of meat in muslin, then a layer of canvass that they secure with a length of hemp rope. They tie a longer piece to the heavy bundle. A stone is tied to one end then looped over a limb of the largest birch tree in the area. They pull the meat nearly twenty feet off the ground and secure the other end around the birch's trunk.

"Well done men," said Macdonald. "Not pleasant work at night or any time, but something that needed to be attended to. The more things we do properly, the more correct decisions we make, the better our chances of success."

McConnell looks into the dark where the dog flesh is still swaying slightly above the ground. He shakes his head and shudders involuntarily.

The wolf speaks once more, a long mournful wail that rides the night wind far upriver, its echo returns moments later, the sound diminished, somber.

-CHAPTER FIVE-

"If you got together a few more men of his stamp, you could get to the moon."

Edward Kenneth Welles
NWMP Commissioner, retired,
commenting on Inspector Wallams Macdonald.

THREE LONG DAYS OF ROUGH TRAVEL finds the patrol nearing the confluence of the Little Wind River and Forrest Creek, and the beginning of a trail that leads over the mountains and down to the Blackstone River valley. Macdonald had expected to cover the distance in two days, maybe a bit less. The place they are aiming for is more than thirty miles upstream from the mouth of the Illtyd Canyon and the campsite made by the patrol following the near-fatal avalanche. And based on the previous days' progress up from Mountain Creek Cabin, and despite the near-fatal avalanche, the inspector was optimistic. The weather has been overcast and cold, minus-fifty, yet the men are used to this. Temperatures at Herschel Island and at Fort McPherson have been known to drop to minus-seventy or lower. Cloud cover is a wintertime fact of life. These two conditions have not been a factor in the lack of progress. McConnell has been doing the trail-making duties the past two days. Galpin's right foot and ankle have swollen from the repetitive and abrasive nature of using snowshoes in deep powder. The joint was nearly double its normal size, the skin bright red and abraded. Some skin liniment and light wrappings have reduced the swelling. This is a common ailment among Arctic travelers. Other than this malady, one that is healing quickly, the group experiences no other injuries or calamities aside from light cases of

143

frostbite on fingertips and the exposed flesh of their cheeks. The skin in these areas has turned a powdery white much like the all-present snow that dominates their lives right now.

"Once frost bitten, always cold," said Fraser in reference to the fact that most frozen flesh, even after it is healed, will always remain sensitive to cold temperatures.

The true impediment to their progress is an inordinate amount of deadfall, particularly between two small unnamed tributaries of the Little Wind that are about fifteen miles apart. The mountain slopes are less severe in this stretch allowing the forest to grow densely. The birch trees are tall for the region, some nearly forty feet. Spruce and jack pine grow in tightly gathered stands forcing the men to cut numbers of them down so the party can move pass.

The downfall is the result of a high wind sometime last year. All of the spruce, pine and lower-elevation stands of birch are facing downhill in a uniform direction as though a massive tornado or similar weather phenomena rose above the ridge line of the front range of the Wernecke's and then crashed down hill at tremendous velocity knocking down and flattening everything in its path before spending itself against a rock escarpment on the eastern side of the valley. Lighter patches on the face of the cliffs indicate impact points from tree trunks and limbs that clearly smashed into the stone with tremendous force. The destroyed forest looks like a graveyard, the shattered and blasted stumps resemble tombstones and the prone trunks the unburied dead left over from a natural battlefield. This must have happened in mid-summer. Many of the birch still have leaves attached to their broken limbs.

The men are forced to either detour out onto the river ice when the bank is gradual enough to allow this option, often to the far bank, a distance of almost a quarter-mile in places. When the gradient is too steep to clamber down, the men must hack a path through the maze of downed timber that is the remains of the decimated forest. Some of the trees are over a foot thick and the wood is as hard as iron because of the extremely slow growing rate in the north country. The tightly-compressed yearly growth rings band together densely, resisting the sharp bite of the axes. Struggling through and over the deadfall is often necessary when their path climbs well above the river with access to the valley floor blocked by sheer drops of many feet. The dogs become restless as they are forced to stop and start, often after covering a distance of fewer than one hundred yards before the tedium of wood cutting begins again. The axe work, clearing the chunks of chopped trees and then maneuvering the sled teams through tight clearings wears on the patrol.

At night setting up camp and eating become work that is drudgery because of the physical and mental exhaustion the men are starting to experience. The never-ending repetitive nature of this journey is wearing on the group. After dinner the four of them smoke their pipes quickly with little conversation and then turn in, immediately falling into a dead, dreamless sleep. They are tiring and now almost always slightly chilled as they climb higher up the steep, narrowing drainage into the mountains. Hands and feet are temporarily freezing but respond to the heat of the campfire. At times the slopes and cliffs pinch in so closely that the men feel like they are traversing the countryside in a tunnel, creating a feeling of claustrophobia. They never see direct sunlight all day. The walls and summits hide the glowing ball from sight. What luminance they do encounter comes in the form of light rays reflecting off sheets of ice clinging to rock faces, the intense glare often blinding men and dogs as they negotiate dangerously narrow sections of trail cutting along precipices high above the Little Wind.

McConnell has not seen any game as he pushes through the piles and drifts of snow well ahead of the others. There is no sign of moose or caribou or even the clumsy porcupines. Not even old tracks or droppings. Nothing except for a lone golden eagle at daybreak that was riding the wind on seven-foot wings heading for better hunting somewhere south, the air slipping over its feathers in a loud hiss. The raptor was no doubt frustrated with the lack of marmots, martins, and other small prey, and was soaring off to more promising territory. In less than two hours it will have covered the distance remaining to Dawson City, something that will take the patrol more than two weeks. Neither the constable nor the rest of the men have spotted any other birds, either. It's as though the land is empty, devoid of all life, a frozen wasteland. This begins to weigh on all of their minds. The feeling of absolute aloneness, complete isolation that makes them feel like they've stepped out of a time and place they recognize, is unfamiliar, frightening. They feel like they are moving through an alien world where they are the only men, a world where except for the nineteen dogs pulling the sleds, there is no other life – that somehow the harsh, white environment that is everywhere and perpetual, eternal is all they'll ever see, all they'll ever experience – an infinite purgatory of frozen dimensions. The four Mounties know better than this, that the depressed states of mind that each of them is experiencing will pass once they clear this canyon and it's Stygian shadows and penetrating cold that seeps into their bones. Once they reach the final pitch to the pass over these mountains their spirits will rise. When they first view the Blackstone Valley stretching far to the west, the Tombstone Range towering in the distant sky, then they'll feel better because they will know that the end the journey is something attainable – that being warm, eating and drinking well with other men is not a crazy dream, but a very real possibility. This awareness pushes them forward, drives them up the ice-bound Little Wind River.

Still, despite, or perhaps because of this knowledge gleaned from years of experience and a profound faith in their wilderness abilities, each man clearly understands that if their progress continues this slowly or worsens, their food supplies, especially those of the dogs whose stamina is crucial to their progress and survival, will grow dangerously thin. They need moose, goat, woodland caribou, anything, to augment their dwindling supplies. Beneath the thick ice of the rivers swim grayling and Dolly Vardon, but despite the proximity of the fish holding in deep pools directly beneath the patrol, this source of protein is unavailable to them. Even if they could chop through the five, six, seven feet of ice, the calories the men would expend doing this while trying to find and then catch the fish would be as much, probably more, than those derived from any fish they might hook and consume.

Following a meal of bannock, dried caribou, dried apples and tea, the men resume their travels a little after noon, the sun shining as it clings to a clear patch of sky barely above the southwestern line of mountains. Galpin is back in the lead about an hour ahead of the main party as they approach the location where they turn up Forrest Creek and leave behind the Little Wind River. He comes upon a fork where two streams of similar size merge. One heads mostly west and the other directly south. The one running west must be a shorter tributary of the Wind River system. It is probably the outlet that a Loucheaux Indian companion, Little Pete, their guide on the previous trip up from the Yukon River and Dawson City, said dead ends after sixteen miles, give or take, against a sheer rock face of more than 3,000 feet, a virtual cul-de-sac – an area of perhaps two square miles of swamp land, ponds, tiny creases of water running to the edge of the cliff and shooting out into space and a dwarf forest of subalpine fir. The Indian worked his way into the place out of curiosity, the desire to find another prime hunting ground. What he discovered was anything but that. Little Pete said that he once shot a caribou that had lost its way and wandered into the place and then was too frightened to return back down the trail to the safety of the lower forest. The animal was "all skin and bones and the meat stringy and tough like old rope," said the Indian. The small basin is very difficult to drive sled teams into, but nearly impassable coming back down because of the steepness and sharp turns of the trail as it "hugs the mountain like a mother holding its newborn," Much of this is extremely narrow where it clings to cliff edges. The perpetual pull of gravity makes controlling the sleds and dog teams a near impossibility. The only place to safely turn around is at the head of this glacial cirque along the edge of an alpine meadow.

"Once in that bad place, you must have much luck to come back alive without all your bones cracked," said Little Pete. "The trail plays tricks. It moves through the trees and looks down on the water and then back a distance into the trees. Then after some miles it comes into the open and is wide and smooth along the side of the mountains, but suddenly it has shrunk and you are trapped with no choice but to go forward. This is three, maybe four miles from the final cliff that blocks out the sky. And then you come around a sharp bend in the trail. The world falls away. The land disappears. All a man can see is that wall of rock, the air below his feet. All he can do is keep going and pray to live. Summer on foot is not so bad. Still very scary. Winter with a sled and dogs might look like death."

Galpin recalls those words exactly as the Loucheaux said them many months ago. He remembers the look of concern, respect and fear on the man's face. Little Pete had made the mistake of going into that drainage on snowshoes a dozen winters past. He ran out of food, lost his bearings in a whiteout and stubbornly pushed ahead. If not for the stranded caribou in the cirque, he would have starved. He shot the animal through the neck and then gorged on the raw meat. There was no wood for a fire that far up in the mountains. As it was they barely made the return trip back to camp dodging avalanches, clinging to the shred of the trail in fierce winds and fighting gravity's pull.

As for the upper reaches of the Little Wind River, no white man has ever been up into that remote country of glaciers, hanging valleys and impassable rapids. Few natives have ever traveled that way, either and their information concerning the steep valley is flimsy at best. The drainage is a place of dense timber and deadfalls, little game and rough rock trail say the Indians. Fraser mentioned one evening while the men were eating that he had spoken with Njootli about the headwaters and the Indian had only said "Bad, rough place. Little game, not even grizzly bear. Only small fish in the rivers. Why bother to go into that awful place?"

So the sizeable flow coming in from the south, the middle of the three streams, must be Forrest Creek, which in summer is more river than creek in its lower reaches. The country looks familiar to the Corporal. The range of taller mountains running east-west about twenty miles away are surely the Werneckes. He recognizes the shapes of several of the peaks including the ridgeline of 7,251-foot Nadaleen Mountain. They can be nothing else. This is the major upthrust of mountains in the area, the geologic feature that should dominate the southern skyline from this vantage point. To his left is a series of rolling mountains, treeless for the final 1,500 feet to their summits, that head to the east. These are the Bonnet Plume Range that heads more north-south than the Wernecke's. Another stream similar in width to the first two works up towards them. Galpin believes that following this course would be an error, that the men would be still traveling along the Little Wind and in essence moving away from their objective and running the risk of disaster. He thinks that the patrol must climb up the drainage that is running almost due south. That this is Forrest Creek and the way to the Blackstone River plateau. He is confident that the stream coming in from the west is Little Pete's unnamed, dead-end tributary and that the other from the east is the Little Wind which twists and winds far back into the wilderness and away from their destination. Looking up the curving course that he assumes to be Forrest Creek his eyes run along high mountains that flank both sides of the drainage. Clouds and winter's low light obscure his view. All looks as it did when he first came through here only in reverse as it should considering the fact that they are traveling in the opposite direction this time. In two, at most three days time they will reach Hart Pass at the crest of the Wernecke Range.

This junction is a propitious place to establish tonight's camp. The men will be arriving soon following a short day on the trail that has been mostly free of obstructions. They can make this early camp, repair any gear, eat well and get a solid night's rest. The corporal will suggest to Macdonald that he dole out a measure of whiskey and that of the quality tinned tobacco for each of them as a way of saying they've done well so far and are nearing completion of the major hurdle in the journey.

While he is confident in his selection of the valley they will move into tomorrow morning, Galpin realizes that this is a fateful decision he is making, perhaps one involving life or death. He has always been sure of himself without being cocky or arrogant. In the past when the inspector has counted on him to decide their way, he has made his selection with no hesitation or second guessing. This time there is the slightest twinge of doubt and this bothers him, the unfamiliar feeling making him uneasy. He shakes his head and gathers himself.

"Get a grip on things, damnit man," he thinks. "Now's not the time to be timid. Pull it together and stand with your first choice. It's always the best one, the one that's carried you through in the past."

In a final effort to make certain he has the lay of the land, the proper direction of travel, lined out, Galpin looks around through all four points of the compass starting east turning through south then west and finally north. He imagines that he is coming up from the south during warmer weather as he's done before. He relives the trip, feeling the warmer air, the sunlight on his face, the sound of rushing water and the smell of pine, moss and the birch that flavor the air with a rich, fecund scent. He recalls how the valley looked to him that autumn not so long ago and he extrapolates those images with the ones confronting him today. Fall. Winter. Warm. Cold. Shades of fall. Winter's complete white. He double checks all of the landmarks. Everything is where it should be and despite the deep mantel of snow, looks as he remembers it. The one hump of hills leading to the high country, a rise of land that divides the two streams that flow west and south does look a good deal like the other located slightly to the east, the one separating the Little Wind and Forrest Creek where he assumes it begins to climb up towards its rugged headwaters and Hart Pass before dropping down along Waugh Creek. Still, he is confident that the first line of hills separates the western tributary from Forrest Creek, that the correct path is up the middle of the three drainages.

He returns to the center of the campsite he has chosen and begins preparing the place for the night. In what seems only a couple of minutes he hears the men and dogs approaching him – barking, exhortations to the dogs, the creaking of leather harness, the ever-present slice of the runners through the snow. The corporal has already built a fire, gathered wood and found two logs to set the stove on. He is in the process of cutting pine bows with his knife for the tent beds when the sleds glide up to him.

"Greetings Corporal Galpin," said Macdonald. He is smiling and full of good cheer. "You've done my thinking for me this late afternoon, I see. And this is a day when I'm amenable to all the help offered me. A wise decision you've made, too. It will be good to establish our camp here before darkness sets in."

The men see to the dog teams while Galpin finishes his chore and also gathers more wood. As Fraser assists McConnell with the preparation of the evening's meal, Galpin describes to Macdonald the course he believes they must take tomorrow, along with the reasoning behind his selection. He pulls out the appropriate map from the leather tube and indicates previous routes taken by earlier patrols. While much of the map is barren, it does offer some information and marginal reassurance that they have a fix on their present location and the future course of their travels. He also indicates the landmarks he has examined at this place and their approximate location on the map. Macdonald nods and only says "I see," and runs his finger along the tracks of previous routes that Galpin has inked in.

"These two abutments look like twins to me," said Macdonald. He is looking up country taking in all three drainages that converge not far from where they are standing. "Are you sure that the eastern-most protrusion of the two is the correct one? The path we embark on in the morning will represent a critical decision on our part, a crucial choice."

"Yes, Sir," said the Corporal. "I've double and triple-checked the surroundings and compared the findings with my memory of the earlier trip this way. There can be no doubt that the middle fork is indeed Forrest Creek and leads to Hart Pass. I believe that this objective is attainable in three days at the most. And I'm convinced that the drainage heading west is the one Little Pete our aboriginal guide described to me on my earlier trip through the country, that it is the one that ends beneath an enormous cliff."

Galpin goes on to explain that in many ways the men will be traveling blind from the standpoint of using the maps. While past routes are on the maps in some detail, and all of their paths are similar, the land including side drainages, mountains and subsidiary trails has never been plotted or, if it has, not with any accuracy. No precise measurements have ever been taken using a sextant. Macdonald has attempted to fill in some of the gaps with his instrument, but on-again-off-again the cloud cover has hindered his efforts more often than not. A wrong turn up an unknown creek could mean the loss of several days traveling time and more importantly the use of vital food supplies. So he makes sure that Macdonald understands that he has used all his resources and experience in choosing the middle drainage.

"I estimate that we are at a little over 2,600 feet in elevation above sea level," said Galpin. "When we left Fort McPherson we were at less than two hundred. Hart Pass tops out at slightly more than 5,000 feet. That's a steep pitch for the final miles to the crest. It'll mean hard going for the dogs and for us, too. We'll have our work cut out for us in the next few days."

"Yes, we will, but we can manage the sharp rise, especially now that our sled loads have decreased significantly from food consumption, especially that of the dogs. So, the middle course it will be," said Macdonald. "And thanks for your suggestion concerning the tobacco and the whiskey. We have enough of the scotch remaining in the cask for a wee dram tonight and still have some left over for a healthy measure when we come down into the

Blackstone valley. A little cheer will speed us on our way tomorrow."

The two men scan the valley where they will be traveling tomorrow. They try to determine the best approaches through the timber and around large rock outcroppings that are visible in the fading light, the rock buttresses casting shadows far across the valley. The carpet of spruce drops down to the streambed in a mantel of green edging towards black shadings that show beneath the covering of snow and are a dull reflection of this lifeless season. After some mild disagreement about the best way through the trees, they settle on a tentative plan of attack.

"Well that's done. Our route tomorrow appears to be a manageable one. After I filled in my log last night, I added up the miles from each day's run and included what I expected to cover today. We've come better than 260 miles from McPherson. That means that there are a little more than two hundred miles remaining to reach Dawson City and nearly all of those are down hill. The difficult part of this trip is approaching an end," said Macdonald. The inspector looks at ease right now. The weariness and worry that was pinching his face and draining the glow from his eyes is gone, replaced by a look of enthusiasm and confidence. Galpin senses the renewed energy in the man and within himself. The two of them have always succeeded in the past. This time will be no different. "It appears that the constables have completed our meal's preparation. Shall we eat, Corporal?'

The two walk back through the snow to the stove and the bubbling stew pot.

Macdonald delays their start the following morning until after dawn. Even with the sun working its way above the horizon somewhere to the southeast, the day is low key, bordering on gloomy beneath a thick layer of clouds that are growing darker as a storm front pushes in from the north up the Little Wind River. He thinks that by giving up some travel time during the early morning darkness, that they will gain distance in the improved light after sunrise, such as it is, and hopefully easier travel conditions.

Within a mile of their last camp the trail starts climbing as it wanders deeper into the forest. This happens so quickly as the dogs forge ahead following Galpin's trail that the men pass the only place to drop down to the frozen creek surface that is a couple of hundred feet wide in this stretch and appears to be easier going than working through the spruce trees. The light is poor. Visibility is limited and featureless in the monotone landscape. Assessing the terrain, trying to locate obstacles, is tough. A narrow opening in the woods and a smooth chute to the stream present themselves briefly then vanish in an instant. Turning around and going back would be difficult. The trees are not large, but fortunately for the patrol they are growing several feet apart allowing passage for the sleds. To reverse their direction the men must unhitch all of the dogs, have one or two of the men watch the canines to prevent squabbles or worse, manually turn the sleds themselves and then put the dogs back in their traces for the second time this morning. This will take nearly an hour if all went well and no fights break out among the animals. Wraith in the lead of the first sled, as usual, appears anxious to continue as he leans into the traces and glances from Macdonald to the track ahead of them and then back again. The hound acts nervous, restless, which is unusual. The inspector decides to continue onward and hope there is a way down to the ice somewhere not too far up the trail.

He had expected to see blaze marks from previous patrols as they moved through the spruce, but there are none – no tan or light gray swatches of exposed wood where the bark's been chopped away by passing Mounties from other years' patrols. He assumes they've weathered over with the passage of time or that he's failed to see them as he concentrates on working his sled through the maze of trees. The only way that they know they are on a trail is the fact that the lower branches have all been scraped off by the passage of numerous large animals. Tufts of tan and white caribou fur cling to sharp broken nubs along the trunks as do hunks of coarser black moose hair. There is little sound here. No motion. No tracks from passing animals. No small birds in the trees. A place without movement or even the illusion of life. Despite the rapid approach of the inclement weather, there is no wind moving down through the valley. The quiet is unsettling to Macdonald. The lack of sounds seems out of place, unreal. Where are the birds, he wonders? Or any other living thing for that matter?

The corporal estimates that they have made perhaps six miles by early afternoon when the patrol stops for food. He has kept within a few yards of the others as he works hard packing snow and pulling down obstructing limbs. McConnell gathers some small pieces of dead wood and builds a fire for a pot of coffee. The smoke rises straight up through the spruce limbs. None of them talk. They wonder how far it will be to a clearing and the night's camp. The sky darkens further and snow begins to fall. Small diaphanous flakes float down lazily at first, then larger ones fall more rapidly. By the time they've finished their lunch the wind has come up and is driving what is now a heavy snowfall down the creek in thick sheets of icy grit that stings and burns the exposed areas of skin on their faces. The temperature is dropping. They all can feel the air growing colder. Macdonald brings out his mercury thermometer and takes a reading. Minus forty-eight. It was minus twenty-seven at daybreak a little over four hours ago.

"Well at least in this cold we won't have to worry about overflow on the creek soaking our feet and that of the dogs when we're on the ice, if we ever find a way onto the ice," he said. "Let's move on. Keep a look out for a way down to the river. Another couple of hours will make a good day's progress and we'll stop for the night. And then the next day will see us summit the pass and drop down into the Blackstone, the land of plenty and the start of the end of our little journey.

They head off into the blizzard. Indefatigable. Determined.

The path they are taking keeps climbing higher and higher above the creek. The only way down is to jump or slide pell-mell down an often-vertical incline dodging rough rock and clumps of tiny spruce. This option is never considered. There still isn't any game. No moose. No caribou. No furbearers like marten, beaver or wolverine. Nothing. No tracks or sign either. The patrol continues mushing their way through the trees, the snow never lets up. The wind increases in magnitude, wailing out of the north and against their backs. Even with all of the exertion, the dogs are covered in a blanket of white, their thick fur preserving precious body heat. They all look like members of a mad, disoriented sled team guided by members of the damned driven to haul their cargo to nowhere or beyond by a merciless master.

Galpin waits for all them to catch up. He is out of breath and tired from making trail. He trades places with Macdonald. Even the men are covered in white. The brief dusk of winter is closing in around the group. Soon all will be darkness within this forest, especially with the cloud cover and snow.

"We are truly a ghost patrol this time around, eh corporal," said the inspector. "I wonder what that Tagisch hunting party we terrified years ago up the Techieca River would think of us now? Their worst fears and primitive fantasies confirmed by our appearance, no doubt. What arcane sacred rights would they practice this time around.

One can only imagine."

They both laugh at the long ago, at least it seems long ago right now in the middle of this frigid emptiness, image of the Indians fleeing at the sight of the Mounties and their horses covered in white ash from the burned over forest. Fraser and McConnell look on in obvious confusion. Macdonald notices this and explains what happened. The constables laugh at the mental image he describes.

"The next open area is where we'll spend the night," said the inspector. "We may have to make do with cramped quarters if we don't break clear of these trees soon. One way or another we'll make do. How far have we traveled do you figure, corporal?"

"I make it ten, eleven miles. From what little I can see ahead of us, I seem to recognize where we are," said Galpin. "The land should open up in less than a mile. There's a fine place to pitch camp. Level. Plenty of wood and we'll have a grand view of the approach to Hart Pass if the weather ever gives an inch and affords us a look see."

With that they set off again, the dogs leaning into the harnesses to overcame the inertia of the inclined sleds. After a few yards they are running evenly at a fair pace beneath the trees. About forty minutes later they break free of the woods and onto a wide, flat expanse. As Galpin has said, there is plenty of room and loads of downed limbs for both the cooking and the campfires. The others are reassured by this accurate estimate of conditions and surroundings. They believe that the corporal knows where they are and has them on the right course.

"The way grows even steeper from here on upwards and the land drops away to our left perhaps three or four hundred feet, but the course is wide and free of obstructions," said the corporal. The other men strain their eyes through the gathering darkness, but all they can see is white that is now tinted indigo in the night. The summit and the pass are invisible. "We've about a half-dozen miles to the beginning of Hart Pass. I recommend that we wait until dawn, as we did this morning, to move on so we can be sure of our way and of keeping to the trail. I don't expect trouble in the form of any of us slipping off the edge and tumbling down the side of the trail. Yet, Forrest Creek is now a long way below us. I think that caution is the way to proceed."

The others agree. After dinner conversation is animated, optimistic. They are nearly out of dried moose meat. The caribou is gone. And most of the dried fish for the dogs has been eaten. But within two days they'll be down on the Blackstone Plateau and have their pickings from the enormous Porcupine caribou herd that has long since completed its annual migration down from the Herschel Island area for the winter. As many as 200,000 animals will be collected in the valley. The men's concern for their dwindling meat supplies will be at an end. They and the dogs will feast until their stomachs feel as though they'll burst. Then it will be on to Dawson City and the world of sidewalks, buildings, people, warmth.

While the other men smoke their pipes and discuss tomorrow's trek, Macdonald indulges himself in some mental exercise as he ponders the major concern, the relative anomaly, that's been troubling him ever since they began working up the Wind River. Where were the several thousand caribou from the Bonnet Plume herd? They normally winter near the Wind River's confluence with the Peel or even along the lower stretches of Forrest Creek. Woodland caribou prefer a forested environment as opposed to the animals of the Porcupine herd that are barren ground animals and thrive on the tundra of the Blackstone valley and the Porcupine River as it flows across the tundra near the Beaufort Sea.. The Bonnet Plume animals should have moved out of their high country mountain valleys in early November at the latest. The patrol would certainly have spotted and killed plenty of them as they passed through the country in late December, all conditions being normal. Did they winter somewhere else? Did some form of disease wipe them out? Certainly the aboriginals couldn't have shot them into extinction. This was not possible. Besides the Indians are always careful to regulate their killing to make sure that there will be plenty of animals for the future. It is now the eighth of January and Macdonald hopes and prays that nothing has delayed or decimated the Porcupine caribou. They've been on the trail for nineteen days and food is growing scarce. Perhaps he should have taken Fraser's suggestions concerning an additional sled and another patrol member or two.

Quickly recognizing the negative aspects of second-guessing himself, the inspector clears his mind and rejoins the conversation with the others. Finally he climbs into his sleeping bag and fills in the day's entry for the log book.

The following morning as daylight reluctantly spreads over the valley, the sun's light the color of ripe crab apples on the lower surfaces of the clouds. The snow backs off from its blizzard demeanor to some extent. The men can see for perhaps a mile ahead of them. Objects like cliffs and trees are barely visible across the canyon, a distance of a quarter-mile. More than three feet of snow has fallen since nightfall. It is a light, powdery accumulation. The dogs have no trouble pulling the sleds through it despite the incline of the trail that is wide enough for a pair of sleds to travel side by side. They make good time and the runners kick up dusty plumes of snow behind them. The visibility never improves. A half a mile. One mile. A quarter mile. Fluctuating but not consistently expanding in distance. Never enough distance to see the end of the valley and the final climb to the pass. Then a squall moves over them, coming out of nowhere, surging over a near ridge, the dark clouds boiling and spinning as they move in on the patrol like a charge from enemy cavalry. It is almost as though the storm is purposely attacking the group in the way that it sweeps down on them. Within minutes the men are unable to see more than a few feet in front of them. The snow falls in dense sheets like a summer's cloudburst turned whiteout. McConnell is driving the third sled and he can just barely make out the shape of Macdonald ahead of him looking like a washed-out shadow moving in and out of view. Fraser is lost from sight manning the lead sled that is headed by the wolfhound. He and Macdonald changed positions in the party's order at the start of the day's travel. Fraser wanted to take the responsibility of working the trail from the front to give Macdonald a breather in the second slot. Galpin, who insisted on breaking trail and leading the way over the pass, is also lost from view.

The flurry of bad weather moves on, passing in less than an hour, riding over the terrain and tearing up towards invisible peaks. It drags cold air behind it. Temperatures are now close to minus sixty. Blue sky is also part of the equation. The land opens up quickly behind them. They can see for miles, down rugged canyons and far off to where the land flattens and drifts north towards Fort McPherson. Traveling the distance with their eyes and minds takes only an instant, but the time since they were last at the post seems like a century ago. Then everything clears off ahead of the patrol. The entire alpine panorama is spread out before them in crystalline clarity.

The view would be considered spectacular by some. Mountain summits reaching to the heavens in all directions. Well below them the spruce forest drapes down along steep slopes dropping to the stream course where dwarf cottonwood and scrub willow and alder take over. A brilliant, partly cloudy sky that shimmers softly blue. Slight breeze. But for the Mounties what they see is terrifying. A nightmare turned real. In the zero visibility of the squall they've unknowingly, blindly moved out along the brink of a precipice. They are lost on the knife edge of oblivion, of sheer death. The trail is no more than five feet wide, a mostly level shelf, created by shifting fault lines in the limestone, more of a mountain sheep trail than anything. And in places it slopes away from the mountain face rising above them and towards the drop-off. This slip of path drops away in a free fall of 2,000 feet. There is nothing all the way down to the valley floor. Not a suggestion of slope. Just the dizzying aspect of clear air. A gyrfalcon circles lazily hundreds of feet below them, the winged predator scanning crevices in the cliff face for prey and also down along the ground for its main food source, the rock ptarmigan that would be nearly invisible in its winter white plumage. The stream below looks like a narrow, serpentine strip of white ribbon that is part of another dimension from an unrelated landscape. There is nowhere to turn around. Barely enough room to inch forward. Sunlight washes up and over the land, the radiance cresting like a golden wave as it washes against and then over Little Pete's sheer 3,000-foot rock face. They've stumbled into the hell described by the Loucheaux to Galpin on the earlier trip. None of them move. They are afraid to. One step might mean death. The dogs are motionless and all of them stare straight ahead. They understand that death is all around them. They are frightened like the men. Wraith stands still. The terror of their predicament roars through them like massive jolts of adrenalin, through both men and dogs. None of the men have ever been afraid of heights. All of them have crawled, climbed and scrambled across cliffs and severe slopes over the years during the course of their various duties and assignments. This is different. This place really is the edge of oblivion. Escape is impossible. Even if they'd consider abandoning the dogs, which they never would, they couldn't. Galpin is able to move forward. And McConnell can inch his way backwards, but the place is so narrow, so confined, he's afraid to try and turn around. The constable would never desert has companions anyway. That's not his way. Nor is it the way of the others.

"We're fucked, men," said Macdonald. He fumbles beneath his parka and retrieves his pipe and tobacco pouch. He calmly fills the worn briarwood bowl, then scratches a stick match on the frame of his sled and brings the flame to the tobacco. He puffs away until it is smoking nicely. Working on his pipe the inspector looks around him scanning the horizon and assessing the situation. The smoke rises in rapid clouds as he nervously draws on the tobacco. The sound of his teeth grinding on the stem sound harshly in the cold air.

The other three are stunned to the extent that they temporarily forget their predicament. None of them have ever heard the inspector use profanity. And none of them would have ever expected him to use this particular vulgarism. And then as casually as though they are standing on the front porch of headquarters, he proceeds to smoke his pipe – contradictions surfacing on the rim of doom.

"Yes indeed, we're fucked," said Macdonald. "There are times, admittedly few, when that rough word is apropos. Our present situation appears to be one of those instances."

He laughs, and looks around him once again. He brushes snow off a small section of the cliff next to him on his right before leaning closer to examine whatever it is he's discovered.

"A find of possibly some significance, gentlemen," said Macdonald. "It would appear that the fossilized remains of a dinosaur have revealed themselves to me here in the middle of our predicament. I must note the location in my journal after we make camp tonight.

"Corporal if this is the valley the aboriginal told you about it would seem that our only option is to proceed to the end of this trail, and I'm being generous with this assessment of our pathway here. I suggest that we all pray as fervently as each of us is capable that the man, what's his name? Little Pete, was right about our being able to turn around when we reach the basin, if indeed that is what we decide we must do. Let's hope that there truly is an expanse of flat ground beneath the wall. Even with that it looks as though we have close to three miles, at least, each way. Not my definition or idea of an easy go of it. We've our work cut out for us today. This is a test from above to see what kind of cloth we're cut from, men. Buck up."

The clattering of stones bouncing off of rock rings and echoes in the canyon. The noise emanates from the cliff across from them on the other side of the creek. The men look in this direction. All of them locate a string of seven Dall sheep making their way across the face of the limestone wall along a trail that is too narrow to be observed by human eyes from any distance. The traverse takes mere seconds before the animals disappear around a dropping bend in the trail that disappears behind a crag shaped like a gargoyle.

"I'll wager that those are the same ones we saw working above us before the avalanche," said Fraser. "There were seven of them just like before, and the lead ram's curl was enormous, well past a full circle, precisely like that of the lead ram we saw in the canyon. I feel like shooting one for the hell of it, but we've apparently angered the gods of nature enough as it is."

"A wise decision, Corporal. The sound of the rifle's report would more than likely bring down every flake of snow gathered by the tons on the ridgelines above us, not to mention part of the mountains themselves in the process. And look at it this way," said Macdonald. "If those sheep can make a go of it, I'd like to think that four of Canada's finest members of its Northwest Mounted Police force are capable of duplicating their efforts.

"Corporal. Make your trail as close to the inside as possible and try and pack the snow at an angle leaning in and away from the edge of the trail," said the inspector. "We'll need every advantage we can gain, no matter how small. Constable Fraser? Do your best to expand upon the corporal's efforts. And keep your voices down. This appears to be prime territory for an avalanche."

The wind is still for now. All is quiet. The patrol is trapped far above the world of relative safety below them and also the one above them that manifests itself in the form of the escarpment that blocks passage to the freedom of the Blackstone valley on the opposite side.

The other three, each in his own way, think 'Doesn't this man ever get discouraged or frightened. He smokes his pipe and carries on about discovering dinosaur bones. And he's giving orders like we're on the parade grounds at Fort Edmonton. We're in a damned hard spot here and if we live to tell about it, it will be a miracle.'

Macdonald taps out his pipe on the sled and puts it away inside his parka.

-CHAPTER SIX-

"The Aurora Borealis, therefore, is the Heart of the Devil. When the Aurora Borealis falls, when it runs close to man, the human brain goes mad and man is seized by the Heart and killed. That is why we are frightened of it and why we reject it utterly and have done so for a long time.

-Dene tradition
as spoken to
father Emile Petitot
1871

THEIR NERVES ARE FRAYED. SCRAPED RAW. SHOT. The men are working carefully, delicately, with extreme caution as they guide the three sleds along the slice of trail scratched on the side of the mountain cliff. The sled dogs, all nineteen of them, place each paw with deliberation. They know as well as their human companions that one misstep will lead to disaster, to certain death. It's been two hours since the squall moved off and in its wake left clear skies that revealed the nature of the patrol's predicament. In that time they've covered at most one-half mile with at least two miles to go until they reach the safety and calm of the basin below the cliff that dominates the western horizon, thousands of feet of limestone towering above the Mounties, the wall looming larger as they come ever closer. The structure seems to radiate hopelessness shaded with malevolence.

Galpin is working in the lead, meticulously packing the snow in a ridge that angles away from the drop-off. He forms the snow as smoothly and compactly as possible with the rawhide webbing of his snowshoes, working fifteen to twenty yards ahead of the group. When he's completed a section, he waves the men onward. There is little conversation, and no yelling for fear of bringing down upon them the wrath of the mountain in the form of an avalanche. Hand signals, gestures and nods of heads pass for communication. The wind puffs and gusts, and seems to be trying to pull the patrol off the cliff, to end this nightmare for all of them with a quick plummet to the rocks below, a fall taking only a few seconds but lasting forever in minds of men and dogs gone insane with the terror of a hurtling, accelerating death, the stone face of the mountain rushing by in a blurred background of gray, ochre and weathered lime before the inevitable collision with the unforgiving earth and the instantaneous transition into the next world.

There are a little more than three hours remaining of what passes for daylight here in early January. At the rate they are progressing, the party will either be forced to attempt a treacherous completion of the vertiginous traverse in the dark or be forced into an uncomfortable bivouac on the side of the cliff. This would entail enduring hours of fierce cold while standing stock still or leaning against the slope. Keeping the dogs under control would be a near impossibility under these rigorous conditions. The animals will grow cold, muscles cramped, backs aching. They will turn restless and finally uncontrollable.

Macdonald quietly calls a halt. He watches as the last hard rays of sunlight sparkle like mirrored rainbows on layers of ice on the far side of the valley. The vision is other-worldly, beautiful.

"Men, darkness will be upon us before long, but I feel it is in our best interests and chances for survival if we press on to the end of this dicey situation," he said. He explains his thinking concerning the dogs and the men's discomfort if they pass the night at a standstill. "We are in a tough place right now. I think that to be fair under these rather uncommon conditions we should hold the matter to a vote.

Majority rules. A tie goes to my plan."

Galpin raises his hand and softly says "Aye," as does Fraser who adds "I'm with you, Sir."

Macdonald turns his head and looks behind him.

"Your plan is good for me, Sir," said McConnell from the last sled. "The sooner we're done with this messy situation the better we'll all feel."

The dogs are silent, motionless.

"Then it's agreed. We have five, maybe six hours more travel if our Loucheaux friend Little Pete's estimate is correct. That is providing we make the same time we have so far out here in the middle of what is plainly a nowhere that men such as we are should ever hope to find themselves in. Obviously life has dealt us a meager hand to play. We'll make the best of the cards we've drawn, eh?"

The inspector breaks into a wry grin. The other three smile at their predicament much the way men of character and fortitude have looked into the face of hard times for thousands of years.

"Lead on corporal. Lead on," said Macdonald.

They inch along the path that shrinks to a little more than three feet wide for the next five hundred yards. The outside runners are within inches of the edge, the steel plates grinding and screeching on patches of bare rock. Galpin leans into the slope and away from the precipice as he steadily breaks trail. The men ease the dogs along the way and cling to the sleds from the rear, willing the heavy things to stay on track. They are unable to work up ahead by the wheel dog and more efficiently direct the sleds with the gee-poles. There is not enough room for men and sleds side by side. Small pieces of rock and ice mixed with snow rattle down on them. Some of the stuff bounces off the men, dogs and sleds and caroms out into the abyss. The sounds of rock glancing off rock echoes faintly up to the patrol.

Darkness begins to settle in around them. The sun's

been down behind the mountains for nearly an hour. The landscape drifts through deep blue shadow before shading to soft purple then nearly black. The wind pushes its way up the canyon. The air grows still colder. Macdonald takes a reading. Minus sixty-six. The lowest yet for the journey. It will be minus seventy or more by daybreak. Fortunately the cut along the rock face widens to a generous five feet, an absolute god-sent reprieve, as the men are exhausted from the intense physical and emotional strain of keeping the sleds and dog teams on track. They are able to slip forward and man the gee-poles, which adds a measure of control and stability to their progress. The trail was clearly formed when a lower layer of the sedimentary rock shifted and moved slightly out from the layer that is level with the patrol. The rock beneath them is darker shading to gray while that rising from their feet for uncounted feet above them is lighter with a tinge of yellow and small scalloped fossils embedded in the coarse surface. A thin band of white quartz with streaks of gold dendrite shot through it parallels the trail. Wraith is working calmly, steadily and powerfully. He and Fraser make a good team. Both are leaders in their own quiet ways. They're sure in their movements yet still cautious as they set an example for the others. If the hound is frightened, he isn't transmitting this fear to the other dogs, who have settled, albeit uneasily, into the tedious, creeping routine of working up the rising incline that inches its way towards the basin at the base of the three-thousand-foot barricade of limestone and granite that dominates the western horizon as it soars far above them nearly wiping out a sky that is now shot through with glowing silver-white points of light from uncountable stars and galaxies. The first-quarter crescent of moon is not yet upon them. The only illumination the men have to chart their course is the faint star light that flickers down on the frozen land. The Werneckes surround them. They are draped in darkness, the snow on the trail is nothing more than a layer of marginally lighter gloom. The wind is a droning whistle as it cuts and streams along the cliff and through large outcroppings that tilt out into the emptiness at angles that clearly defy gravity and natural logic.

Macdonald looks ahead and above him. He is able to discern where the basin begins. Shelves that must support mossy, hanging gardens in warmer times are visible climbing like gigantic steps to a line of stone that appears to level out and run to the cliff base, perhaps a distance of more than a half mile. As the trail bends sharply around to the right or north he sees that the level area winds back into a narrowing valley that is formed by the main abutment and the slope of the mountain that they're clinging to right now. 'Perhaps,' he thinks, 'a moose or a few caribou are holding up that way, trapped by the weather and their fear of coming back down. Perhaps.'

There is, at the most, another mile to go before they reach the sanctuary of the basin. That is the length of this high altitude torture that stands between them and the basin. Not a great distance when running through the forest far below, but way up here hanging on to life, that lone mile takes on immense proportions in all of their minds. The wider trail allows them to increase their pace slightly. They keep moving in silence.

"God, give us two more hours of safety," said Macdonald to himself, to the unfathomable space to his left. "That's all we need."

All of the men are now suffering from severe frostbite in their hands, feet and along the exposed parts of their faces. They've been unable to take even the smallest of breaks from managing the sleds and dogs to warm their hands against their bodies. The pain of freezing fingers was intense at first, but has been gradually replaced with a chill numbness. Feet are frozen stumps that feel nothing. Several of their fingers have turned to black ice. Cheek flesh is darkened or raw and bloody red where the dead skin is peeling away. They ran out of dried fruit days ago, and even the apples and currants they ate at the beginning proved insufficient when it came to providing necessary amounts of vitamin C, especially when factored in with the near-deficiency of the vitamin in their regular diets back at McPherson and Herschel Island. They only delayed the onset of the disease. They are beginning to suffer from the embryonic symptoms of scurvy including swollen and bleeding gums, loosening of teeth, sore and stiff joints, and bleeding beneath the skin. The obvious deterioration of their health makes reaching the Blackstone valley paramount in importance. If they fail to do so within a week, two at most, they will die.

The wind continues to grow stronger, gathering itself in hurricane bursts that buffet men and dogs as the air slams over them while shooting up from the valley, then smashes back into them from the opposite direction after bouncing off the rock wall. One tornadic shot causes McConnell to lose his grip on the back of the sled, thick gloves slipping free of the ash frame. He tilts backwards and his feet go out from under him. The constable crashes to the ground, head and shoulders hanging out into space. Only his back and legs provide the friction necessary to keep him from tumbling to the valley floor. Despite the closeness of the night he imagines that he can see a pile of shattered rock lying in a jumbled maze along the creek a couple of thousand feet below. Tilting his head slightly he sees the black bulk of the 3,000-foot wall looming as a massif that has a malignant identity all its own. McConnell's world is now measured in vertical distance that is portioned in thousand-foot increments. From visualized death in the distant streamed to the possibility of salvation if the patrol can negotiate over this ultimate barrier rising so far above him into the night sky, his existence claims a mile of linear space. His life is now measured by this brief distance that also takes on a vastness that he thinks may be beyond his ability to surmount.

He pulls himself gingerly up into a sitting position, then leans and rolls forward onto his hands and knees, a posture he holds for nearly a minute as he gathers himself before standing. He resumes guiding the sled. The six dogs instinctively stopped when they sensed McConnell's loss of contact with the wooden frame. They've waited for him to regain control. Now they pull against the harness with a force that moves everything forward slowly with no jerking or weaving. Within minutes he has closed the lost distance between himself and the next sled.

Macdonald peers into the darkness watching the progress that Fraser and Wraith are making. He can see the beam of Galpin's torch flickering along the trail up ahead. The inspector often chided the corporal for spending his hard-earned money on what he called "a device devised by modern lunatics," especially in light of its name – The O.T. Bug Friendly Beacon Electric Candle. Galpin had grinned and said "Some day this little lamp may well save our lives. The Bug Friendly may show us the way in a tight spot. You'll see, inspector." He'd laugh at this weak pun and his superior would groan. Macdonald had forgotten that the man even had the torch, let alone packed it for this trip, until now as he watches the yellowish cast of the beam move back and forth a few feet ahead of the trail breaker.

'It's amazing what makes me smile and think of the comfort of headquarters when I'm holding court with death,' he thinks. 'A damn torch does this to me. Quite curious.'

The wind has not diminished. If anything, it's increased in strength. The temperature is now past minus seventy. One benefit of the rigors of this stretch is that the exertion helps keep man and dog from freezing solid.

The Inspector watches as the corporal signals a halt with an upraised hand that is illuminated by the torch. He begins aiming the light back in the direction of the others when the most ominous of sounds comes from the first sled. The familiar screeching of the iron runners resumes unexpectedly at an astonishing increase in volume and pitch. This is quickly joined by other noises – dog claws scrabbling on rock, Fraser yelling, the painful creaking of stressed wood.

"Hang on there, you bastards! Pull! Hard! Now!"

Then more metal and claws scratching and tearing against limestone

"Damnit! We're lost!"

The torch beam swings onto the ungodly vision of Fraser suspended almost completely over the side of the cliff, feet dangling in space, bare, frostbite-blackened hands clinging onto the back of the sled that is pointed at a sixty-degree angle into the air, two dogs lifted off the ground and swinging madly from their harnesses. The other beasts are frantically pawing and pulling to maintain their tenuous hold on the trail. Wraith is lunging and heaving into the traces with loud, hoarse grunts, but the hound's fierce efforts only delay the inevitable. In an instant that never seems to end in the eyes and minds of the other three men, Fraser, followed by the sled and then one dog after another, slides from the defile over the precipice and swiftly out of sight.

Gone.

The last image Macdonald sees is Wraith's long legs and wide paws clambering for purchase on the cold stone, huge fangs exposed in a grim expression of survival, and knowledge of approaching death. He disappears like he was never there to begin with. All is silent for a moment. then the mortal wail of Fraser and a deep bellow from Wraith echo and resound among the stone walls. This is followed by the explosion of the disintegrating wood from the sled as it crashes against the boulder field and then the softer "whomps" of living bodies slamming into the ground.

All of this reverberates throughout the valley, gradually dying away. It is replaced by the moaning of the relentless wind that seemed to die down in unconscious premonition of the approaching disaster, but resumes its force now that man and dogs have vanished in the black emptiness.

Fraser is gone. Wraith is gone. The other six dogs and the sled with most of the patrol's dried meat are gone. They've all come so far and are so close to the end of the extended cliff-side, horror-filled passage. The fate of the lead sled seems cruel, unfair.

Macdonald is speechless. Galpin sobs. McConnell stands staring down into the abyss. He can't see anything, but keeps looking all the same.

Long minutes pass. There is no sound coming from down below along the valley floor.

As if on a subconscious command, Galpin begins working slowly ahead breaking trail in the light of his torch. Macdonald eases his team forward. McConnell turns his attention back to his sled and dogs. He begins to follow.

Less than a mile of this ordeal remains. The survivors, men and dogs, are determined to make it.

They push on.

~ ~ ~

The fire, as small as it is, burns with surprising brightness in the brutally cold dark – surprising considering that its fuel consists of twigs, frail limbs and small broken pieces of the trunks of subalpine fir that are no more than two inches in diameter. The wind has died down, an uncommon situation in this mountain basin. The constant blow that has driven the men crazy with its punishing presence since that arrived, began to ease up around noon and died away completely a few hours ago. The snow clouds that have closed in upon and surrounded the cirque where the men are holed up have moved over the mountains along the southern ridgeline. All is silence except for the sound of the wood burning in crackles and hard pops when the tiny knots in the wood ignite, and that of the men eating. The temperature at more than 4,000 feet above sea level has been seventy below or lower for days.

After escaping the cliff edge, they hauled everything across the flat over what must be the frozen surface of a large pond, and around mounds of rock on their right that form the southern extremis of a glacial moraine perhaps forty feet tall. A still life waterfall of thick ice drops down from a notch in the wall and near the base of the cliff widens pushing tons of pulverized rock into a massive mound of olive green shading to bronze and slate at the base. Snow is packed and wedged into narrow gullies formed by erosion over the centuries. Otherwise the wind has swept the feature clean of snow. Hillocks of frost-heaved moss and other plant growth made the footing treacherous. The men persevered finally reaching the slight shelter afforded by the wall and a pile of broken rock. Establishing camp took hours. The survivors were dejected and exhausted. The dogs were nearly dead from their efforts and the stress. The remaining Mounties were, and to a large extent still are, emotionally beyond despair or fear for their own lives. They grimly cling to one goal, the completion of their assignment. One way or another they are determined to reach Dawson City even though one of the bags of mail and dispatches was lost with Fraser and his sled team. Macdonald has quietly and subtly worked at restoring all of their spirits. He's been successful to the point where they are now able to go about their daily chores and to also coherently plan for the future.

Macdonald, Galpin and McConnell are searing hunks of stringy dog flesh over the flames. The last of the dried moose and caribou was eaten eight days ago. The dried fruit went the day before that. They've been camped, stranded, locked in by the weather, in this basin for ten days. Gale-force wind, white-out blizzards that reduced visibility to zero and intense cold made moving even a few feet an ordeal. The tarp they used to make a crude shelter is covered in snow. Their time has been spent gathering wood from the sparse supply present in the basin. When not hunched up around the fire, they are curled up beneath the tarp and their bedding trying to cheat the unrelenting cold that seems the cut through their skin and dig into the marrow of their bones. The misery of the weather is constant. They burned the last pieces of ash and birch from the sleds either the day before yesterday or the one before that. Time has lost meaning and importance in this empty, sterile environment that is devoid of any life or stimulation. There is little flour left from a bag secured on McConnell's sled, some tea and a handful of tobacco. Everything else is gone. They finished off the last of the whiskey the first night here in a somber send-off for Fraser and the dogs. As exhausted and morose as they were on arrival, the liquor did little more than dull the physical pain from the cold and put the smallest of dents into the emotional turmoil that runs a constant circuit from their heads to their stomachs and back.

The men pitched camp back from the edge of the basin and beneath the cliff trying to obtain any shelter possible from the elements. After toasting their departed comrade and the dogs, especially Wraith, they retired to their sleeping bags that were set next to each other beneath the remaining blankets and then a worn canvass tarp, The other one is suspended just above the ground in an attempt to conserve heat by minimizing the air space between the men and the fabric. The bed of pine bows is thin, reflecting the sparseness of the trees that cling to life in this harsh, high-altitude environment.

The men are suffering from extreme frostbite. Their feet, ankles and lower legs are swollen. Even the thought of removing their footwear is painful. The leather gear would need to be sliced off. Unlacing would do no good because of the enlarged condition of their extremities. The dead skin on their hands and faces that has not sloughed off is dark blue, black. Some of it hangs from them in ghastly patches and strings. The symptoms of scurvy have intensified. Galpin has lost several teeth. All of the men's joints experience a constant burning ache. They are in a state of semi-lassitude, nearly devoid of energy. Only their intense will to live, the desire to survive their predicament to complete the journey, keeps them going.

McConnell shot the twelve remaining dogs the other morning with the rifle. Twelve shots. Twelve bullets in twelve dogs' heads. By the time they were killed, the animals were dissipated, sickly looking. They have one box of shells remaining. Skinning and butchering the meat was an awful, mean task that all three men worked at for the better part of a day. As they did so, they chewed on pieces of the raw flesh that was already freezing as they worked away. The taste was not as bad as the men had anticipated. Their hunger, driven by meager rations of flour and the dried game, overcome any reservations and aversions to eating the remains of animals that had toiled faithfully for the men over the past month. Survival strips away any civilized conventions with ruthless efficiency. The canine protein rallies them to some extent. Each of the three has lost a great deal of weight. Their blood-shot eyes bulge from shrunken sockets. Cheek bones rise sharply. They are without even the suggestion of any remaining body fat or muscle tone. Over the past weeks their bodies have been digesting their muscle tissue for sustenance. As the dogs were shot, the others looked up from their nests of snow and then sunk back to sleep or unconsciousness. They were too worn out to muster any fear about the fate of their companions, or their own for that matter.

"Galpin and I will attempt to make our way up the scree slope and then along that rising ledge that appears to lead over the crest of this wall," said Macdonald. He gnaws on the tough meat. "It will be a steep go of it, but the way offers our only chance of escaping this place and of survival. We'll leave at first light in the morning. Hopefully the wind will be down.

"As we discussed earlier today, I believed, and still do, that it would be best if all three of us went for the summit together, but considering the state of affairs here, I left that decision to each of you. Each of you has the right to make his own choice. I respect and abide by what you've each decided."

The inspector slowly reaches into the pile of sticks in front of him and lays several on the dwindling fire. The dry, weathered wood bursts into flames. A stream of sparks shoots upwards towards the stars and the intense aurora that is flashing shades of blue and crimson that none of the men has ever seen before. The cliff behind them, the trees, the snow, all of it shines in a colorful glow that intensifies to a surreal imitation of daylight then drops back to subtle luminescence and back up again. The northern lights shimmer and flow like the light of the men's campfire.

"Since you have expressed your desire to remain here to try and find some game, we obviously will leave the rifle and remaining ammunition," said Macdonald to McConnell. "We'll have no need for it and the piece's weight would be an added burden. We will take some of the dog meat, two-thirds of the tobacco, and two of the blankets."

He reaches inside his parka and pulls out the tin of imported tobacco.

"Fill your pipes with the last of our good blend."

179

He passes the container to McConnell who packs his pipe and hands it to Galpin who does the same before giving it to Macdonald. The men light their pipes with burning sticks from the fire and smoke awhile in silence. They resume their conversation. Words are the last solid connection with their past lives of now understood and appreciated purpose and comfort. They are stripped bare of even the small niceties and necessities of living like coffee, shelter, decent food. All they have left to them is this talk, their words, each other. Their voices still hold life's enthusiasm even though they've been reduced to rasping whispers from the cold and tiredness. Despite these austere conditions, what they have remaining seems like a lot. Each of the men in his own way is grateful.

"Thank you, Sir," said McConnell in a barely audible rasp. His throat is raw, painful from a cold and breathing in the bitter weather. "If I can bring down an animal, hopefully a moose or a caribou, the meat will restore my strength. As things are now, the way I feel, I don't believe that I have sufficient strength or stamina to attempt the summit with you. I'd be a hindrance, if anything, and I don't wish that.

"There is plenty of shelter here for game to over-winter. A small spring pushes through the far edge of the pond we crossed on our way in. The water must percolate up from a subterranean reservoir. I saw that there is some plant growth around the edges of this source barely beneath the thin ice at the spot. It is possible that what I saw was the track of a moose. I intend to work the flat beyond those trees where it twists around behind the mountain. I feel that some sort of game is holding in that nook out of the wind. If I kill anything, I'll eat until some of my strength is restored before following in your tracks. I'll bring as much meat as I can carry."

"Good man. God's speed to you," said Macdonald. "Let's make the last of the tea."

He empties a pouch that holds mainly powder and stems of the Darjeeling into the only pot they have. It is filled with boiling water made from melted snow, the one resource they have in abundance. After the mixture simmers for a bit, he pours equal measures into three cups. The men clutch them for their warmth and take quick, small sips.

"There never has been any doubt in my mind that I've had and am having the privilege to serve with three of the finest men ever to wear the colors of Northwest Mounted Police," said the Inspector. "Constable Fraser died serving his country. Doing his duty with honor, determination and dispatch. You two have done nothing less. Whatever our fate, whatever the outcome of this patrol, we have done our Service proud. It is my hope that Galpin and I succeed in making our way over the divide and down into the Blackstone valley. Based on a measurement I shot recently, we should be roughly parallel to John Glisch's cabin on the other side of this obstruction. The structure will be within our grasp if we scale this damned mountain. Perhaps another six miles would remain. That crazy Pole trapper has wintered down where the Hart River comes quite near the Blackstone for more than a dozen years. He may well be our salvation."

"I've heard many tales of his activities," said Galpin. "I was told that he once tried to domesticate a pair of wolverines that he'd snared. While he was out one day running his trap line, the two animals destroyed his cabin, knocking over the wood stove in his absence. The coals started a fire that destroyed nearly all that his possessions not to mention his shelter. When he returned there was nothing remaining but ashes and empty cans that the animals had torn open with their teeth and claws. They'd even managed to dent the stove somehow. He never saw either of the wolverines again."

"That would be the man I'm speaking of," said Macdonald. "he's known for his eccentricities such as the one you've described, but he is also renowned for his generosity and helpfulness to his fellow man. If we reach his place, you and I will rest and build up our strength so that we may return for McConnell's rescue, provided he hasn't arrived already. Glisch will help. He always assists those in need with whatever he has and in whatever way he can."

McConnell nods and throws a couple of sticks on the fire. He thinks, 'Maybe we'll survive this, maybe we won't. But each of them in his own way is determined to struggle for life to the end no matter how painful or grizzly in nature.' This heartens him. He is convinced that he spotted old moose tracks beneath the snow a couple of days back while gathering wood. They were heading in the direction he described to the others. If he can bring this animal down and feast on the meat, all will be well. He is sure that he will lose several toes and fingers to frostbite. Feeling left his hands and feet days ago. Thankfully, because of the extreme pain that the crystallized blood cells were causing him. At this point, amputation of the digits will be a small price to pay for survival, warmth, a hot meal and a soft bed. He smiles at the thought of these images.

Galpin notices the man's expression and smiles, too. He then looks over at the inspector, laughs some and launches into the story of he, Baptiste and the albino moose of years ago in Alberta west of Edmonton.

When he's finished McConnell said "Nothing in this wild land seems uncommon, strange or unbelievable to me anymore. I've seen too much in these past years at McPherson and on this journey. After all of the struggles and dangers of this journey, our lack of food, the incredible cold, Fraser and the dogs...well...nothing really seems very real to me anymore. I have a difficult time of it trying to discern between my dreams and imagination, and what is actually happening. An albino moose, even an albino grizzly seems totally within the realm of possibility after all that I've experienced in the Arctic. White is white in this country. This place in winter is a ghost land."

They again discuss more concerning their earlier decision not to try and go back down the trail. They all feel that this would be too risky, that the remaining sled team would never make it and neither would the men. The exertion, steepness of the grade and narrowness of the way would all conspire to finish them off. Even if they did manage to succeed, they would have more than two hundred miles and many days of trail to cover before reaching Fort McPherson. None of them believes that they would have the slightest chance of completing that journey.

"Even if you fail in your quest for game, you will have the last of the meat from the dogs," said Macdonald. "I regret deeply that things have come to the point where we must eat the animals, but we had no other choice. Absolutely none."

Boiling and eating the harness along with the webbing of their snowshoes is an option, a last ditch attempt at prolonging survival. The three of them know that this would be pointless and distasteful. An acquaintance of Macdonald's became so desperate, so hungry one lean winter that he tore out the animal parchment windows of his cabin and boiled them for sustenance. The man survived the ordeal but vowed to the inspector that he would never even consider attempting to make a meal of the parchment, or for that matter, his babiche snowshoe bindings either. Rawhide, sinew and dried gut will never be a part of that particular individual's diet again. He vowed to die of starvation first. The unspoken possibility of consuming one of their own, of eating the flesh of the first man to die, flashed briefly through each of their minds when they first arrived in the basin after grimly completing the trail passage along the cliff face. This was immediately discarded with shared glances, a look of understanding among men who have endured hardship together few others would even understand. Their thoughts are as one now and they are in complete agreement on this subject. Suicide from a .30-30 bullet in the head is preferable to cannibalism. Tales and rumors of desperate men driven to this odious but understandable behavior circulate about the north country constantly, as do rumors of aboriginal tribes that kill not only each other but white trappers and prospectors as well. And these stories tell in often gruesome detail of how the natives impale their victims, often while they're still living, on a large stake and slowly roast them over a bonfire, hacking off pieces of meat from the screaming individual. Eating human flesh, eating each other has never been an option, has never been an issue.

"Men, when we get out of this and are in Dawson City, we will still have some rough road to travel," said Macdonald. "My feet and hands are in dire shape. They are of marginal use and will do their job, but fortunately they are frozen beyond feeling or the pain that goes with the condition. My extremities will serve their purpose in tomorrow's climb and descent to Glisch's cabin, but I fear that I will loose parts of me to the surgeon's saw. I suggest that you prepare yourselves for a similar fate."

"I've already worked that over in my head,' said McConnell. "I can deal with whatever happens."

"Sir, I, too, have considered the possibility for the past week," said Galpin. "This patrol is the end of my active duty with the Service. I will be physically unable to perform my duties. I understand and accept that. I know that I will be taken care of by the Service. I'm at peace with that end of our situation."

He looks each of the other two in the eyes before continuing.

"I wish that this assignment had gone easier. I share a great deal of the blame for our difficulties. Most of it I fear. I am in a large way responsible for Constable Fraser's death. I'll never get over or forgive myself for this. Losing a hand or foot means nothing to me now."

"Ease up on yourself," said McConnell. "I knew George better than anyone. He would have been the last person to lay blame on you or any of us for our predicament. He understood the nature of our duty and life in this unforgiving land. All of us have done the best we are capable of. There is no blame involved in any aspect of this assignment. Constable Fraser died performing his duty. He lived the life he and I had always talked of when we first joined the Service years ago far south in Alberta. Be at peace with this, corporal."

"Fine sentiments constable. Ones that I concur with," said the inspector. "Our life of service to the Police is often a tough one that at times can appear unjustly harsh and cruel. We freely chose to be posted in the Arctic and we volunteered for this patrol. None of us has reason to complain or bemoan our fates, whatever they may turn out to be.

"I listened to your argument for choosing this last stretch of trail and saw the land as you did that day when we made our plans to come this way," he said. "This country appears different, unfamiliar in the winter, especially when traveling from the north and not up from Dawson City. Njootli, for his own mysterious reasons, decided not to be our guide. Not to accompany us in our endeavors. He may have made no difference even if he had been with us on this trip. You, corporal, have performed your tasks admirably, conscientiously and with honor. Constable Fraser knew this right up to the instance of his death. There is no cause or need to feel guilt with regard to the performance of your duties."

"Thank you, men," said Galpin. He puffs on his pipe. "My burden has eased some."

They finish their pipes then crawl beneath the open bags and the tarp. They are able to share what little body heat they have by lying next to each other as they shiver through the interminably long night.

~ ~ ~

McConnell works around the base of the tongue of rock deposit that is the leading edge of the glacial moraine. He left camp at dawn after bidding farewell to Macdonald and Galpin who headed for the base of the scree slope in the opposite direction he is traveling. The men shared a last meal of the dog meat and cups of hot water. Then they shook hands, embraced and went their separate ways, hopefully to be reunited in a few days. If all goes well, McConnell will be rejuvenated from feasting on a moose that he hopes to shoot today, and the other two will be recuperating at the cabin of the John Glisch. Perhaps the trapper will be working his way to the summit of these mountains from the Blackstone valley in the west as the constable does the same from the eastern face.

Considering the condition of his feet, McConnell is moving through the deep powder easily, the webbing of his snowshoes sinking down several inches in the lush softness of the fresh snow. Getting up in the mornings is a painful experience. Areas next to frozen skin burn as though hot needles are being shoved into the flesh. Joints are stiff. Sharp pain shoots through them until they have loosened some. Overall weakness makes every movement an effort. The constable is haunted by maddening thoughts of lying in a warm feather bed for days on end, a nurse serving him hot food and tea.

In thirty minutes he's nearly past the moraine, the pile of crushed stone rising many feet above him. He stops to catch his breath and survey the terrain ahead of him. He looks up to the crease of sky between the mountain peaks that form the valley and fantasizes that he is watching three ravens gliding to the north towards the open flat lands near the Beaufort Sea. But instead of black plumage, the large birds are pure white. The birds become real to him and he thinks he can hear the air sliding over the surfaces of their wings. They sail swiftly out of his imagination's view. At his feet he sees what appear to be large, though faint, depressions in the snow. Dropping down on one knee, he examines them.

Nothing is definable in the twilight conditions. He feels like he is wandering through the starkest and coldest of dreams. The marks in front of him could be tracks or are they only slight dips in the accumulation of snow that has fallen steadily and heavily in the last days. He keeps looking, but the thick overcast dims the daylight and turns everything to monotone, flat, lacking form. He could ponder the situation for hours, but decides to pursue what he sees as though they are game tracks, those of a moose. Wasting time is a luxury he can't afford right now.

McConnell follows where he believes the suggestion of a trail is heading. He is moving away from the glacier and the wall, and moving parallel to the flanks of the mountain they came in on, the one with the wicked trail that claimed Fraser and his dog team. While following the faint marks, the more he becomes convinced that this is the trail of the moose that all of them hoped and suspected was holding here all along. Maybe his eyes are indeed fooling him. The tracks are not becoming any more defined, but nor are they slowly fading away into nothing. Believing that a moose became trapped on the narrow path along the cliff, unable to turn around because of its bulk, and then found its way into this small valley is not that much of a stretch, especially for a lonely, solitary man suffering from extreme hunger. To extend the belief a step further to the possibility that the animal chose to stay in this place rather than risk the trail again does not require much of a leap of faith. Desperation often spawns visions of such minor grandeur. McConnell continues his pursuit.

Stopping to scan the terrain ahead of him again he thinks he hears the faintest of calls. One that is simultaneously deep-throated and high-pitched. "Eeeooww." He can barely hear the wild voice that seems to drift across the frozen land as though made by a ghost, like the sound a thick limb makes when it breaks away from the trunk of a large tree, the sound muffled by layers of the softest of Egyptian cotton. He holds his breath and tries to capture the call again.

Nothing.

He waits.

Nothing.

McConnell follows what he imagines to be the direction of the moose. This takes him on a course that clearly opens out of the scrub subalpine trees and ends at the edge of the cliff. He has the animal trapped. The only way it can try and escape is to come directly back towards him. An easy shot head on into the creature's chest. Freedom is blocked in by the mountain slope on the left, the drop off directly ahead and the moraine to his right.

He clears the trees. The precipice is at most a couple of hundred yards distant. He peers across the thick snow over the featureless landscape.

There. Directly ahead.

Something standing alone.

Not more than fifty feet from the edge.

He sees the animal. Enormous. Over six feet at the shoulder with a rack that spans seven. The moose must weigh nearly two-thousand pounds. The beast is entirely white. He thinks that its dark brown hide must be covered with snow.

The bull stands motionless.

McConnell closes in, a shell chambered, gun at chest level. He's ready.

Closer.

The animal does not move.

Closer.

He sees that the white color comes from is its thick, shaggy hair. Not a covering of snow. Galpin's albino moose is now here in this high mountain cirque to provide meat that will save his life. He stops and breathes quietly, regaining his wind so that his aim will be steady.

No motion from either of them. He's within forty feet. He raises his rifle and sights in on a spot right behind its shoulder.

He fires and hears the "whap" of the bullet slamming into flesh.

The moose leaps forward in a spray of white powder. The creature is enormous. Beyond belief. It charges for the cliff.

The man pursues, moving quickly on his snowshoes.

Leaping as though taking flight, the moose soars out over the abyss above the distant valley floor. An arc of snow trails in the animal's wake.

McConnell keeps running and snaps off a shot as he tries to close the distance between the two of them.

Then he leaps over the edge after the animal. He finds himself floating and falling through space with the moose so close now, only a few yards ahead and below him.

Both of them sail through the air in gravity's control.

Falling. Floating, Soaring.

Forever.

~ ~ ~

Macdonald takes the lead as the two of them pick their way across the slope of shattered and cracked rock. Even though the scree slope is covered with a thick layer of snow and the men are wearing snowshoes, large jagged hunks of the stone trip them up or block their passage. The angle of the hill is nearly forty-five degrees. In the weak light picking out an obstacle before it becomes a hazard is problematical. Their goal is a rounded notch located three-thousand feet above them in the wall that appears nearly vertical from this far below. The sheer presence of the limestone face towering above them is at once intimidating and formidable. Neither of them has ever attempted to conquer a geologic feature of this magnitude. They've accomplished free climbs of a hundred feet and more while on assignments in the wild, and the traverse of the lethal trail that lead into this out-of-the-way hanging valley. But nothing like what is before them now. They will be hanging on to the slimmest of tracks on the side of a truly awesome mountain wall that at the end of the climb will see them nearly three-thousand feet above the basin floor. Both of the men spent hours scouring the lay of the cliff with Galpin's binoculars as they sat on a brief rise next to camp. The inspector and corporal worked out a route that appears from down below to lead to the summit, to give access to the crest and a hopefully benign way down to the Blackstone.

"I can't see any other way but the slice of ledge winding to the opening," said Galpin. "It seems like this is part of the fault that formed the shelf that leads into this place. It must work along beneath where we camped then wind below the scree before surfacing along the wall. The band of copse winds parallel to it as it did on the way in here."

They discussed the situation some more, but the conclusion was still the same. They will be forced to negotiate the face of the cirque along that slip of ledge. The way is exposed, dangerous and the only one that the men can locate. This scratch in the rock running along the cliff is the one blemish or feature that offers the slightest chance of escape. Success is at best a fifty-fifty proposition, but the slim odds are preferable to freezing and enduring the constant gnawing in their stomachs from starvation.

Macdonald is carrying a small canvass rucksack that has rations of the cooked and now frozen dog meat, some water, the binoculars, a hand axe and lantern. His watch is wrapped in a handkerchief and stored in an inside pocket of the pack. They each have knives in scabbards attached to their buckskin leggings that are now well-used with all signs of quilled and beaded adornment long-since worn away. Galpin is too weak to manage even this small additional weight. They've each wrapped a ragged blanket about their shoulders, the thread-bare garments providing more psychological protection from the cold than anything else.

The scree ends approximately twenty-five hundred feet below the top. From the southern end about a half-mile from camp the fault in the stone angles steeply upward running north and crossing perhaps two hundred feet beneath the notch. The angle of ascent is sixty degrees or more in places. From below the opening a wide, slanting fissure filled with stone and boulders and slabs of rock balanced precariously against each other accesses the space between the cliff walls that rise on each side forming a large natural gun sight. The course along the fissure appears to be as narrow if not more so than the trail that brought them into the basin. They have no idea what they'll find on the other side – another precipice, or a gradual slope down to the river. When they begin this portion of the climb they will have to remove their snowshoes, strap them to their backs and proceed wearing nothing but their worn mukluks. The leather on the footwear is worn through in places from abrading while strapped to the snowshoes. Their other moccasins and mukluks were packed away in Fraser's sled. Galpin estimates that the total distance they will need to cover is a little more than two miles counting the hike from camp to the base of the cirque. He figures that they can negotiate this distance in three hours, four at the most. This will give them nearly two hours of passable light, even in this overcast, to scramble down to lower ground and build a crude shelter in the spruce forest for the night before continuing on to Glisch's cabin.

Both of them realize how weak they've become over the long weeks of constant travel in extreme conditions as they struggle over the pieces of rock and through the deep snow. Normally they would skim the surface of this debris moving with ease and making good time. Drifts of a dozen feet or more have accumulated in depressions along the slope's surface. Now they are moving in slow motion. Lacking any feeling in their feet and very little in their hands, they misstep, stumbling and sinking up to their hips in places. They help pull each other out when this happens. After two hours they finally reach the lower end of the fissure. They are out of breath and dizzy from fatigue.

"That took twice as long as I expected, Sir," said Galpin. He is gulping air. His eyes are slightly glazed.

"Yes, but we should make better time along this crack in the cliff," said Macdonald. "The way seems mainly clear of snow, ice and rock,"

He notices the deteriorating condition of his companion, but realizes that the only choices they have are to remain here and die of hunger and the cold or attempt to fight their way to the top, much of this on their hands and knees clinging to any rough spot or crack for purchase. So far the wind is down. At least that's in their favor. He takes off his pack and grabs a hunk of meat for each of them.

"Chew this. Then we'll proceed."

Macdonald is also tired, weak and winded, but he vows silently to continue no matter what the obstacles or apparent outcome. When they finish eating, they remove their snowshoes and help each other secure them to the other's back with rawhide laces they brought along for the purpose. The weight is an obvious hindrance. Trying to cover the final miles on the other side of the mountain through snow that will no doubt be deeper because the western flanks have sucked much of the moisture from passing storm fronts coming down from the northern sea would be impossible.

"It's time, corporal. Let's be off," said Macdonald. He claps Galpin on the shoulder, turns around and begins the slow, severe scramble to the distant notch that now show itself as a small patch of lighter gray against the gunmetal color of the limestone and schist wall.

He wonders how far it is to the fissure? A mile at least from the top of the piled rock they're resting on now. The first few hundred yards go well. Both of them lean away from the edge and into the wall, moving one foot ahead of the other with great care. The shelf they're working is nearly four feet wide along this stretch and the slope is gradual. Then the angle increases to as much as seventy degrees in certain pitches.

"Hands and knees now, corporal," said Macdonald. "Focus on the ground in front of you. Don't look down. I don't intend to. We'll make it."

Galpin is running on reserves he never imagined he possessed. He estimates that they have less than a mile now. He's exhausted to the point of being beyond pain or fear. He follows the inspector as he has for years, the pair scratching and clawing their way up this steep pitch that runs for hundreds of feet. The going is slow. The wind starts to come up blasting against them from the northeast. The gusts batter the two as they hang low on the ledge. Macdonald took a reading this morning. Minus seventy eight. If anything, the air is colder now. The sun has been out of sight since they began working up the scree. The height of the wall dominates everything in their vision, even obliterating the rays of sunlight. They've toiled, strained their eyes searching for handholds, in deep shadow for hours.

The way levels out and they are able to stand, providing relief for burning muscles and inflamed joints. Shuffling along they cross this stretch easily. A barrier of jagged stone that has sheared away from the main face provides shelter from the exposure that is now over two thousand feet. They are able to move about in this area without fear of falling. They stretch their arms and legs and bend over to work the kinks out of their lower back muscles. The light is bad. They can barely make out the campsite set next to the spruce trees that have lost all definition this high up, looking like nothing more than a black mat stretched over the snow. The tarp is a tiny rectangle. The fire pit is invisible. Somewhere down there is McConnell hunting for a moose, caribou, anything. Or maybe he's already killed, skinned and butchered an animal and is roasting it over a fire while scanning the wall for signs of his companions. But they are specs against the enormity of the cliff and impossible to spot with bare eyes. They can't see him either.

Macdonald examines the stone at his feet. In a sheltered corner not more than a few feet square he spots a scattering of small dark pellets. 'Sheep,' he thinks. And in the powdered limestone residue he sees wedged-shaped tracks blunted at the tips. 'Definitely sheep. If those creatures passed this way, we can accomplish the same.' That sheep have walked where they are is good news to the inspector. He smiles for the first time today. His normally positive spirits are restored.

"We're getting this done," said Macdonald. He points out the tracks to his friend, who also smiles and nods. They look up and see that the fault narrows to three feet, if that much, and that the angle is the most severe yet. "We've our work cut out for us, corporal. No doubt on this issue. Hands and knees again. Crawl forward as best you can. A few inches at a take if need be. The fissure looks as if it will afford us a place to rest within a pile of boulders I see from here."

He points out this feature, large rock piled to form walls on three sides with the cliff face making the fourth. The men can rest there out of the weather.

"As you say, Sir," said Galpin. "I'm with you."

They labor on. The wind rises to a gale. The ledge is nothing more than a wisp of rough rock now that leads to the shelter of the jumble of stone beneath the notch, a place of respite that seems far away, almost unreachable. Moving one foot is an effort of concentration and delicate caution consisting of gently sliding the outside hand along the edge of the incline. Then the outside knee is brought up followed by the inside hand and then the inside leg. A foot at a time. Sometimes several minutes are spent to gain twelve inches. Then some time is needed to catch their breath, to regroup, before repeating the process. Neither man looks over the side at the airy death patiently waiting for them, for any slight mistake they may make. They are a part of the limestone now. They've blended and molded themselves into the slight variations of the surface as they creep along. Their focus is one foot directly below their faces. That tiny space represents the dimensions of the world they perceive right now. Macdonald hazards a glance a few feet ahead every twenty feet or so. All he notices is more of the same steep, scary-as-hell climbing that is growing more difficult as night begins to take hold of their surroundings. The cliff has become a Chimera of horrific proportions. The glow of stars and galaxies and the ever-present shadowy flickering cascade of the aurora lights their way like a staircase in a lunatic castle.

"We'll have to bivouac among the boulders for the night," said Macdonald as he stares ahead examining the course and estimating the distance remaining. "This is taking much longer then we estimated. No surprise, but we're nearly done. We're going to succeed here."

Galpin only nods even though Macdonald can't see the movement. He's already moving forward. The inspector knocks a large stone from his way. It clatters off the wall well below him shooting sparks into the darkness. The sound of its fall is washed away on the wind, but he follows the rock's path by the bursts of light it makes crashing against the escarpment.

The wind rips and tears at the two as they lean into the cliff face willing themselves to stick to the rock. The light is weird, ghastly. Sheets of alien blue, rose and orange sweep across the wall and the men. They've become nothing more than living machines whose soul purpose, whose only goal, is to move forward and upward one foot at a time. They continue the climb. They're far beyond hunger, cold, and pain. The aurora is all around them. The light in some arcane twist of natural fate has dropped down out of the heavens and is glowing in eerie radiance along the ledge, in the open space below them, whirling above their heads. Fantastic color dances and skips across the stone. The entire valley, the entire world for all they know, is shimmering in a riotous storm of light.

Macdonald pushes against stone. He looks up. The pile of boulders. A way to the less slanted piece of ground within some of the larger rocks is a few feet off to his right.

"This way, corporal," he said. "Bear right."

Twenty minutes and maybe twenty feet later they are huddled in the shelter.

"We've made it, Sir. Even though I had my doubts at times, deep down I knew that we'd accomplish this. I have no idea what's happening. This light all around us. I've never experienced such things before. Perhaps I've gone mad."

"I understand," said Macdonald. "Our world is filled

with wonders that we can't explain or describe. As long as I live I'll always hold the vision of all of this in my mind. This place is dangerous to the point of wickedness, but ever since we've stepped into the basin I've had the strong sensation of being beyond our world and our time. Like you suggest, perhaps we've gone mad." He takes off the rucksack and pulls out some meat. "Have this, then we'll rest for the night. Tomorrow we make Glisch's. The way will be easier."

Galpin removes his mittens and takes the meat. His fingers are ravaged, ruined. He cradles the meat in his hands as though they are a fire-blackened bowl and brings the flesh up to his mouth. He takes the small portion in and tries to work at it with his remaining teeth. He manages to extract some juice mixed with his saliva. He swallows this then spits out the chunk. He is thirsty, extremely thirsty, but their water is frozen. He scoops up some gritty snow and lets it melt in his mouth. Then he repeats the process before leaning back and losing consciousness.

Macdonald hooks his arms beneath Galpin's shoulders and drags him farther back into the shelter. The nearly comatose man mutters "Thank you, Sir. I'll have more strength tomorrow," then closes his eyes. Galpin's feet point down to the valley far below like a human compass searching for the direction home. His arms are crossed upon his chest as though he is in deep thought, or corpse-like repose. Macdonald pulls his remaining blanket from around his shoulders, rips the tattered wool in half and covers the other man.

He sits down and imagines that he is in front of a roaring blaze that is turning out intense heat. He stretches his bare hands over the flickering flames dancing in his head. He thinks of his years in the Arctic, all of the experiences, all of the mistakes he's learned from and he wonders what happened this time.

He says to those flames "Where did I go wrong?

197

Where?"

After a period of time not measured in minutes or hours, he rouses himself.

'If I don't do something now, he's finished,' thinks Macdonald. 'I've been through a great deal with this man over the seasons. I've always been able to count on him. He's never wavered in the face of hardship. Not in the past and not this time, either. He's my friend. I'll leave the meat and the rest of my blanket with him. I can make the notch and be at the cabin by dawn.'

He wakes Galpin to bare consciousness, and shouts into the roaring wind what he plans to do. Then he settles the last scrap of wool blanket around the man's shoulders and lower face like a shroud.

Galpin nods. His eyes close. He is almost dead.

Macdonald begins moving up through the boulders and loose rock. In the wild night glow he can see the notch not more than one hundred feet above him. The last fifty of these are open, totally exposed to the elements.

The wind is rushing against and up the face of the cliff with terrific force, actually providing some lift for him. He moves hand over hand, foot by foot. He breaks out onto the bare rock that is sloping towards the opening now so close to him.

Stars blaze with unfamiliar brilliance. Lights of the aurora shine insanely. The world, the one from his past, is gone, never existed. There is only the distance of stone to climb. Nothing else.

A meteor sizzles across the sky trailing a stream of hot green sparks. The flaming object seems to clear the notch by mere feet as though it's lighting Macdonald's way.

He looks above him and reaches with a bare, withered hand for the opening, fingers extended into the night.

-EPILOGUE-

"The lifelong vigil for redemption, each show of faith in the face of torment and doubt is a reprieve from madness."

- Inspector Wallams Macdonald,
NWMP,
Herschel Island
Winter 1909

NJOOTLI AND KUNNIZZI wind their way over the slopes of the Illytds that flank the river canyon at the location where Macdonald and his men were nearly done in by the avalanche. The trail is clear and smooth. The steps of many animals and men wandering this direction over the centuries has worn the path down to stone and packed dirt. Without many feet of snow to hide the way, the course over the mountains is direct and little more than a stern hike for men in good condition like the two Indians. The dwarf willow that lines the river and feeder creeks along with the ground cover beneath the spruce is beginning to take on the intense spectrum of autumn color on this late-August afternoon. Fall comes early to the northlands. The leaves of ground-hugging huckleberry and black currant bushes are already crimson and flaming orange. The berries have turned to near black and are beginning to dry out, their surfaces already wrinkled. Mosses are taking on ruddy overtones that seem to mimic the rusty striations of quartz in exposed bands of rock among the hillocks that rise up around the two Loucheaux. Game is plentiful along the river corridors – moose, woodland caribou, marten, porcupine, beaver. Overhead strings of waterfowl are already heading south as they flee the never far away presence of approaching cold weather, vicious winters. Honks, quacks, and whistling wings fill the air. Within a couple of hours the two men attain the junction of the Wind and Little Wind rivers and the unnamed valley that the Mountie patrol wandered into last winter. The remains of burned logs and branches are scattered in a rough circle. Poles chopped and trimmed for the tents rest on the ground, the cut ends already turning gray from exposure. Desiccated droppings from the sled dogs lie scattered about the trees thirty yards from the fire circle. Already clumps of grass and moss have reclaimed some of the darkened earth. Sparrow's-egg Lady Slipper, white blossoms shining, grows along the edge of the trail leading into the camp. Loucheaux men often wear the flowers next to their heart with a strand of hair from the woman they love attached in hopes of attracting the maiden's attentions.

When Macdonald and his party failed to arrive in Dawson City by mid-February, officers at the NWMP headquarters became alarmed. They waited three more weeks hoping that foul weather and other problems along the trail had delayed the patrol's eventual arrival. By the first of March the commissioner ordered action taken. On the tenth of March a search party of six Mounties led by Sergeant William Taylor along with four dog sleds set out to try and locate the men. Taylor, who has already made the run in both directions in past years, retraced the route from the opposite direction Macdonald had taken, running from south to north. He was convinced that Macdonald and his men were holding either at Glisch's cabin or at Mountain Creek Cabin. He couldn't convince himself, actually couldn't conceive, that any harm had come to men as skilled as those who made up the latest patrol. There was far too much experience and wisdom, not to mention prudence, for anything disastrous to have befallen Macdonald and the others.

Within a few days they reached Glisch's place along the

eastern bank of the Blackstone. The man was repairing a number of his steel traps when the group arrived. The day was warm for March, at the freezing level. The trapper was sitting on a stump in his shirt sleeves in the sunlight.

"Never saw a sign of them," said Glisch. "I was expecting a patrol to arrive from one direction or the other, eh. The men always stop for the night and I put on a good feed with roasted moose and a stew of grouse and ptarmigan that I make. Then we drink from my whiskey keg. It's a tradition as you know Sergeant. I seem to remember you having some drinks here once or twice in past years. I look forward to the camaraderie."

They both smiled at the memories.

"It's bad doings that no one's seen hide nor hair of that patrol," said Glisch. "I've spoken with that man Macdonald. He's a good one. I'd travel with 'im. The fact that he's gone missing is a worrisome sign. I fear that all you'll find, if you turn up anything, is bodies. My prayers go with those men and with you. Even the best can die young if the fates will it to be so."

The party spends the night and eats well. They drink from the trapper's store of whiskey but the night is more somber than cheerful. All of them worry over the patrol's fate, something even the effects of good whiskey cannot totally overcome.

They depart early the next day. After working up Waugh Creek and over the Wernecke's at Hart Pass, Taylor and his party push down Forrest Creek to the Little Wind and finally the Wind and on to the Peel River. All of the streams are still frozen over. Ice-out is two months or more distant, sometime in mid- to late-May.

They search well up into the forest that lines their path, tracking along well-used game trails and clear stretches between the trees that grow mostly crowded together. They find no signs of Macdonald's patrol, not a trace, which is already being referred to as The Lost Patrol in newspaper stories that are flashing around North America and Europe. Members of the Northwest Mounted Police meeting with failure, possibly death, is electric news in Canada and much of the rest of the world. Taylor explores a number of side creeks and river valleys but pays scant attention to the winding drainage that eventually gives way to the cliff-side trail and the hanging basin that wreaked havoc with Macdonald's group. From his vantage point at midday, from almost the identical location where Galpin and the inspector made their decision in January in the dark of early evening, the sergeant has the benefit of a sun that is already much higher in the sky than it was when the winter patrol came through the country. Taylor decides that the drainage is an obvious dead end and that a man of Macdonald's experience would never turn up that way. Far in the distance, at what he believes to be the head of this valley, the top edge of the great wall is visible as a hard, purple line cutting evenly across the sky. No man would consider crossing the mountains over that escarpment. Taylor turns his attentions in other directions. Hoping that the men may have tried to return to Fort McPherson and are holed up at Mountain Creek Cabin, the search party heads there. The cabin is in good shape. Mounds of snow surround its walls. Inside the place is tidy. All they find is a note attached to a table with candle wax that reads:

"All is well this evening. We bring in the new year in fine spirits and excellent health. We expect to arrive in Dawson City within three weeks, four at the absolute most. Men and dogs are in are fine condition. Food supplies are adequate. God's generous will to all."

Inspector Wallams Macdonald, NWMP – December 31st, 1910

Taylor sets up camp at the cabin. For the next ten days he and his men divide into separate parties of three retracing their steps back to the south along the Peel then up the Wind River as far as the Illtyds. They also strike off into the trees in all directions for many miles around the cabin. They find nothing. They manage to shoot moose and woodland caribou along with grouse to supplement their stores of meat.

Taylor decides to move on towards Fort McPherson. They reach the camp along the headwaters of the Caribou River, the site of the wolves' slaughter of the moose. Frozen bloody hunks of hide and fur along with piles of bones – rib, leg, skull – partially covered by melting snow, litter the ground. They discover the remains of a large bonfire and the two logs used to support the Yukon stove. None of Taylor's party have ever observed such carnage of wild game, such hideous destruction. The place resonates with death and fear, but there is no sign of the patrol. They scour the surrounding woods for any indications of the men or trouble. They find none. Taylor pushes on to McPherson, his search-and-rescue trip unsuccessful. After resting for three days, he loads fresh provisions and returns to Dawson City along the same trail. Again he and his men find nothing. They pay no attention to the unnamed valley heading west into the heart of the mountains, the one Macdonald and Galpin selected. The drainage has already been considered and discarded as a possible course used by the lost party. Besides, there is no sign or indication that Macdonald and his men or anyone else has ever traveled that way. The only sign of the patrol has been the note found at Mountain Creek Cabin. Nothing else. He makes the return trip in twenty-nine days, nearly a record. and relays his findings to the commissioner. A report is filed and copies are sent to Edmonton, Regina and Ottawa. Updated stories make the newspaper rounds from Montreal to New York to London to Glasgow. The Lost Patrol remains a well-publicized mystery.

For the next several months every Mountie, trapper, prospector, trader and native in the region keeps his eyes open for any sign of Macdonald and his men. None of them find anything. Its as though the patrol vanished from the face of the earth. Their disappearance and apparent deaths are both devastating, considering the reputation of the NWMP in the Arctic and across Canada, and a mystery. Men die and their bodies sometimes are never found, but an entire patrol with sleds and dogs vaporizing into thin air? – especially one led by a man of Inspector Macdonald's experience and character. And Galpin, Fraser and McConnell have excellent reputations earned through years of solid duty in the Service. All of this is beyond reason to seasoned Arctic campaigners. The initial excitement surrounding the news of the tragedy slowly dies away, but the whereabouts of the patrol is on the minds of everyone living in the Yukon and Northwest Territories. Conversation around campfires or in saloons eventually turns to the subject. A great deal of whiskey and ale is consumed discussing the matter. The fate of these men could well be the fate of anyone in the north.

"I have a bad feeling here," said Njootli. The day is warm. Puffy cumulous clouds ride the sky. Above them herringbone bands of cirrocumulus drift in from the north. "The spirits tell me that a terrible mistake has taken place. A wrong path was taken. Men have starved and frozen in the lonely wind. They have died up this way."

"They traveled up the creek to the trail on the side of the cliff," said Kunnizzi. "I warned the corporal of this place, as did Little Pete. The two ways look like brothers during the lower miles. The evil path can fool a soul into believing that it is traveling a course that it has covered before. 'Always bear to the west,' I said to him. 'Forget about the silly bother of left or right forks. That is how a man gets himself very lost in this country.' I always worried that if he ever walked this way again the power of the bad canyon would call to him and lead him to death."

"The Mountie Taylor reported that he looked up this way towards the dark wall, but he understood nothing. His eyes were unable to see what we see with our hearts today," said Njootli. "It is where they died. This is clear. We need go no further. I am satisfied. Our people know of this place and will not go here out of respect for the land and the souls of the dead men. This is the place of their eternity. It is not for us. I will not disturb those spirits of men I cared for."

Njootli and Kunnizzi take out tobacco and pipes. After packing and lighting them, they offer the smoke in all four directions of the compass and to the sky and the earth. When they are finished smoking in silence they put the pipes back in their pouches. At the junction of these three streams that proved to be a deadly confusion for Macdonald and Galpin, they mark a series of trees close together and pointing in the proper direction so that no doubt can exist about what course to take. Then the Loucheaux work upstream on the west side of Forrest Creek. Every hundred yards or so they hack wide blazes at shoulder height into the trees. Stripped of bark, the inner wood shows bright tan in the daylight. They continue on their way fulfilling their task and an unmade promise to Fraser, McConnell and the other two Mounties by marking the trail as it winds for its entire course up and over the mountains. They continue up the trail to Hart Pass. Next they proceed down Waugh Creek. From here the way is clear. The recognizable mountains on the western edge of the Blackstone plateau rise in the distance like massive beacons that point the way to civilization. They ford the Hart River and move across the tundra. The first caribou recently come down from the north, along with moose, graze in the open that drifts for miles beneath the Arctic sun.

In the distance grizzlies work along the slopes that define the valley. The bears gorge on berries preparing for the lean times of winter.

When they reach the Blackstone, the two follow the river downstream to the Peel and their village.

Thank you for reading.
Please review this book. Reviews help others find
Absolutely Amazing eBooks and inspire us to keep
providing these marvelous tales.

If you would like to be put on our email list to receive
updates on new releases, contests, and promotions, please
go to AbsolutelyAmazingEbooks.com and sign up.

ABOUT THE AUTHOR

John Holt is the author of 21 published books including *Where Paradise Lay, Death in a Live Forest and Fly Fishing Montana, Stalking Trophy Browns, Montana Fly Fishing Adventures, Yellowstone Drift – Floating the Past in Real Time, Arctic Aurora – Canada's Yukon and Northwest Territories, Hunted: A Novel, Coyote Nowhere – In Search of America's Last Frontier,* and *Fly Fishing Adventures – Montana.* His work has appeared in such publications as *Men's Journal, Fly Rod & Reel, The Denver Post, American Cowboy, Audubon, Jeep Magazine, Big Sky Journal, E – The Environmental Magazine, Art of Angling Journal,* and *Outside.* He and his wife, photographer Ginny Holt, live in Livingston, Montana.